Secrets of Lina's Necklace

Sara Noor

CONTENTS

SECRETS OF LINA'S NECKLACE I

1 THE DEPARTURE 3

2 LEAVING ANANKE 8

3 SETTLING DOWN IN EARTH 12

4 AUNT AMEERA'S DEPARTURE 21

5 BOARDING SCHOOL 26

6 LINA'S FIRST DAY 33

7 SCHOOL LIFE 41

8 REMINISCING 51

9 A NEW TERM 65

10 SOMETHING GOES MISSING 69

11 THE NEXT MOVE 77

12 ANOTHER STRATEGY 83

13 A PHONE CALL WITH FAMILY 103

14 TIME TO GET IT BACK 112

15 ANOTHER BREAK IN 117

16 TIME FOR THE TRUTH 125

17 CONFRONTATION **132**

18 AUNT AMEERA INTERVENES **141**

19 A LONE MISSION **145**

20 TIME TO FIND PEACE **153**

21 REFLECTIONS AND GROWTH **160**

ABOUT THE AUTHOR **171**

ACKNOWLEDGMENTS **172**

Secrets of Lina's Necklace

1

THE DEPARTURE

Lina woke up to the warm rays of the triple suns peeking through her window, casting a kaleidoscope of colours across her room. As she stretched, her fingers drifted towards her crystal necklace, its crystalline beauty resting serenely against her chest – the sacred necklace of Ananke, a symbol of her planet's ancient power and protection.

Each child is given one from birth, individual and

unique to each of them, to harness the country's energy around their neck. Lina's necklace features small white crystals with a larger coloured stone at its centre. They were all smooth and emitted a gentle glow based on the energy in Ananke.

Ananke was a planet of breathtaking wonder, a haven of life teeming with diverse flowers and greenery. The fields were turquoise, and the trees were green with brown leaves. This made it an ideal home to a peaceful, enigmatic species, including flying creatures that could be ridden from town to town.

Two of Ananke's three suns shone brightly into Lina's eyes, making it hard to get back to sleep. She lay on her back, wondering about the day ahead.

"Time to come down sweetie," her mum called.

"Okay, I'll be there soon," Lina replied.

She got up reluctantly, and after getting dressed, Lina headed to the kitchen, where her mother was preparing breakfast. The aroma of a sweet, flaky pastry filled the air. Lina's stomach growled in anticipation.

"Good morning, sweetie!" Her mother said, giving

Lina a gentle hug.

"Today's a big day. Your father and I have an important meeting with the Safety Council. You know our job is to help protect Ananke and its inhabitants."

Lina's eyes widened. "Is it about the mysterious threat?"

Her mother nodded.

"We'll know more after the meeting. But don't worry, we'll always keep you and Dina safe. "

Lina's younger sister, Dina, bounced into the kitchen, her curly hair bouncing with each step.

 "Can we come to the meeting, pleeease?"

Lina chuckled.

"No way, sis. We have school today. "

As they finished breakfast, Lina's father, Jax, entered the kitchen, his expression serious.

"Girls, we need to talk."

He looked at his daughters with a mix of concern and sadness in his eyes.

"We've received a distress signal from the edge of our galaxy from a planet called Noctora. Your mother and I will need to leave immediately to investigate and resolve the situation."

Lina's heart skipped a beat.

"But what about us? What will happen to us?"

Jax placed a reassuring hand on Lina's shoulder.

"You and Dina will need to stay with Aunt Ameera on Earth. It's the safest place for you right now. "

Dina's eyes widened in disbelief.

"EARTH! As in Planet Earth? As in, another planet far, far, faaaarrrrr away from here? No, thank you! Nope! No way!"

"This is just temporary, Lina," her dad replied.

"Okay, great. So I'll be in my room during that time with all three suns shining on my face daily," Lina replied sarcastically.

"Lina, this isn't a debate. The citizens of Ananke may not be safe at this time, so to protect you as best as we can, it's important you stay hidden, out of harm's way completely, especially as you girls are associated with us." Her father said sternly.

"But I don't want to leave Ananke! I have friends here, I know where everything is, and it's comfortable for me here." Lina replied.

Lina felt a pang of worry. She had never been separated from her parents before.

"How long will you be gone for?"

Jax hesitated.

"We're not sure. But we will stay in touch through the communication device. You will be safe with Aunt Ameera. You met her when you were younger. She's very kind, and I know you girls will be in good hands with her. And don't worry, you will enjoy getting used to Earth's customs, cultures, and food. I hear they have a dish called fish and chips, and you have to put vinegar on it."

"Fish and chips? Do they eat fish? Ew! My best friend is a fish species, and I would never eat her - yuck! What a strange place it sounds." Lina said.

"Sounds funny to me," said Dina. "I want to see the fish and chips now."

"See, children, you will have a great time. Now go pack your bags; it's important we get moving now," their father said, moving them along.

2

LEAVING ANANKE

The next few hours were a blur of activity as Lina and Dina packed their bags and said goodbye to their friends and family. The sisters were nervous but felt glad to have each other.

As they boarded the spaceship, Lina felt a lump in her throat.

Their mother hugged them tightly.

"We'll be back soon. Take care of each other." Jax smiled, his eyes misty. "And don't forget to enjoy your time on Earth. It's a beautiful planet. "

*****

Lina and Dina watched Ananke disappear in the distance as the spaceship took off. They were alone now, but together.

Lina gazed at the stars streaming past the spaceship's windows, her mind wandering back to the vibrant planet of Ananke, her home. A mix of emotions swirled within her. Nostalgia washed over her, remembering the warmth of Ananke's suns on her skin in the mornings, her friends' laughter, and her parents' wise guidance.

The journey to Earth was long and tiring, but Lina and Dina were excited to explore their new surroundings. Aunt Ameera greeted them warmly at the spaceport and drove them to her cosy home in the suburbs.

"So, girls, nice to see you after so long. I'm sure

you'll settle down here in no time. You can freshen up once we're at the house, and I'll show you around town. You must be hungry after that long journey," said Aunt Ameera.

"Thanks, Aunty. Sounds good," said Lina, in a sombre mood.

"Anything on your mind, Lina? I'm happy to talk about things. Remember, a problem shared is a problem halved," said Aunt Ameera, smiling as she looked in her rear-view mirror towards Lina.

"I'm just tired, as well as nervous about Mum and Dad and everyone in Ananke," said Lina, her head resting on the window.

The cityscape had faded into the suburbs, where endless rows of trees streamed past like shooting stars.

"Trees are brown here, with green leaves," she whispered to herself, smiling a little.

"It's the opposite in Ananke."

"Don't worry, girls, this isn't the first I've seen a distress signal in Ananke. I've seen this happen before, and I doubt it will be the last," said Aunt Ameera reassuringly.

"Your parents know what they're doing. Before you know it, you'll be back home."

"Sounds good," said Lina, smiling.

"I already miss the sun's warmth on my face," she said, her eyes closed, daydreaming about the suns.

"Oh, yes, about that. Can you see that sun over there? Well, Earth only has that one sun, but I can assure you, it gets rather warm in this part of Earth........ for a few months of the year," she coughed a little as she said the last part of her sentence.

"One sun? Ohhh," said Lina, planting her face into her hands.

"Don't worry, darling, we must be grateful even for this one sun; otherwise, it would be very dark all the time, right?" she said positively.

"What do you think, Dina? Dina? Dinaaaaa?"

Aunt Ameera quickly looked over her shoulder and noticed Dina fast asleep on her armrest.

"Okay," she whispered.

"You girls rest. It's another hour before we arrive home. Exciting things have yet to begin for you girls."

3

SETTLING DOWN IN EARTH

The next few days were a whirlwind of new experiences—trying Earth food, learning about human customs, and adjusting to the planet's unique energy signature. Lina missed her parents dearly, but Aunt Ameera's kindness and warmth made the transition easier.

Her home, a serene oasis in the suburbs of Hampstead, enveloped them in warmth and comfort. Soft sunlight filtered through the lush greenery, casting dappled shadows on the walls as they settled into their new routine.

"Wow, I'm so glad we're finally settling in," said Lina, taking a bite of her sandwich.

"I was worried I'd never get used to this Earth food."

"I know, right?" replied Aunt Ameera.

"But you're doing great. And I'm glad you're enjoying the sunshine. It's perfect weather for a trip into Central London."

"Yay!" Exclaimed Dina, bouncing up and down in her seat.

"How exciting," says Lina enthusiastically.

As they walked through the bustling streets of London, Lina and Dina's eyes widened in wonder.

"Look, Aunt Ameera! A big red monster!" exclaimed Lina, tugging on Aunt Ameera's hand.

"Where? Where?" asked Dina, bouncing up and down.

"There!" said Lina, pointing to a giant red bus rumbling down the street.

Aunt Ameera chuckled.

"That's not a monster, dear. That's a bus. It's a way for people to get around the city."

Lina and Dina looked at each other in amazement.

Lina took a photo of the London skyline.

"I'm going to send this to Mum and Dad."

"Make sure to send one to me, too!" chimed in Aunt Ameera, smiling.

The girls marvelled at the history and grandeur as they passed by famous landmarks like Buckingham Palace and the Tower of London.

"In Ananke, we have the Great Crystal Caves," said Dina.

"But this is amazing!"

Aunt Ameera smiled, happy to see the girls embracing their new surroundings while cherishing their home memories.

"Girls, we're going to visit the River Thames," said Aunt Ameera, smiling.

"We'll just take a stroll along the riverbank and

enjoy the view."

Lina and Dina excitedly followed Aunt Ameera to the river. As they walked along the bank, they gazed out at the water.

"Wow, it's so big!" exclaimed Lina.

Dina nodded.

"And it's so…….so dirty!"

Aunt Ameera sighed.

"Yes, unfortunately, the river is quite polluted. But it's still a beautiful sight."

Lina's face scrunched up in concern.

"Why is it dirty, Aunt Ameera? Don't people take care of their home planet?"

Dina added,

"In Ananke, we love our home and always keep it clean. Why wouldn't people here do the same?"

Aunt Ameera explained,

"It's a complicated issue, girls. There are many reasons why the river is polluted. But it's true, people should take better care of their environment."

As they continued their walk, the girls noticed people littering and throwing trash into the water.

"Look, Aunt Ameera! They're making it worse!" exclaimed Dina.

Lina's eyes widened in dismay.

"Why are they doing that? Don't they know it's hurting their home town?"

Aunt Ameera shook her head.

"Some people don't understand the impact of their actions, or they simply don't care. But we don't copy that behaviour. We have to spread awareness and promote change."

The girls nodded in agreement.

*****

Later that day, they sat down at a cosy Italian restaurant. Lina and Dina couldn't wait to try more new foods.

"I'm so excited to try spaghetti!" exclaimed Lina.

Dina nodded enthusiastically.

"Me too! I saw a picture in a shop, and they looked

long and hard!"

Aunt Ameera chuckled.

"That is what pasta looks like raw. You have to boil it so that it softens before eating it. Now, let's order, and I'll show you how to eat it neatly."

After ordering, Aunt Ameera demonstrated how to twirl the spaghetti around a spoon to be neat. Lina carefully followed her example, but Dina had other ideas.

Dina took a piece of spaghetti and slurped it up, leaving a mess of tomato sauce around her lips. Lina burst out laughing.

"Dina, you're so messy!"

Aunt Ameera laughed too.

"Well, I guess that's one way to enjoy spaghetti!"

Dina grinned, the sauce still on her face.

"What? I'm just having fun!"

Lina teased,

"You look like a creature who's been feasting on berries!"

Dina playfully rolled her eyes.

"Hey, at least I'm not boring like you, Miss Neat-

and-Tidy!"

Aunt Ameera smiled, happy to see the girls having so much fun.

"Well, I think we can all learn from each other. Lina, maybe you can loosen up a bit, and Dina, maybe you can try being a bit neater!"

The girls giggled and continued enjoying their meal, making happy memories together.

"I have an idea, girls. From time to time, we will try different cuisines together. How about that? Suggests Aunt Ameera, keen to show the girls the wide variety of foods London offers.

"I love that idea. I can't wait to see where you take us next time," replied Lina.

"I'll keep it as a surprise then," said Aunt Ameera, smiling.

*****

Aunt Ameera's gentle guidance soothed the girls' frazzled nerves as they navigated their new reality. Aunt Ameera's expressions turned serious as they sat in the cosy living room surrounded by vibrant artwork and plush cushions.

"My dear ones, keeping your origin a secret is essential. Your parents' mission, your necklaces, is connected to a world beyond this one."

Lina's hand instinctively rose to the crystal pendant, now symbolising her connection to Ananke and the mysterious threat looming over her family.

"Why must we hide?" She asked.

Aunt Ameera's eyes locked onto hers, filled with a deep understanding.

"The universe is full of wonders, Lina, but also dangers. Your necklace is a beacon, a sign of your heritage and the power that lies within. We must protect you and keep you safe from those seeking to exploit the power."

"Okay, Aunty, we understand," the girls said.

As the days passed, Lina grew more aware of the necklace's presence, its gentle glow a constant reminder of her connection to Ananke. She began to sense the subtle vibrations, the way it pulsed with an otherworldly energy. The glow, which was once a soft whisper, now shone brighter, a warning of the increasing danger that threatened their family.

Dina, ever the curious one, watched with wide eyes as Lina's necklace flared to life.

"What's happening, Lina? Why is it glowing like that?

Lina's heart raced, and her mind raced with implications.

"I think it's trying to tell us something wrong, Dina. A warning, maybe, or a message from Mum and Dad."

Aunt Ameera's expression turned grave, her voice low and urgent.

"We must be careful girls, something must be happening in Ananke that is beyond our control. We must stay safe and cautious."

4

AUNT AMEERA'S DEPARTURE

Aunt Ameera's eyes fluttered closed, her face a mask of concern, as she listened to the urgent message from Ananke. Lina and Dina exchanged worried glances, sensing the gravity of the situation. The air was heavy with unspoken fears.

"I must leave, my dear ones," Aunt Ameera

announced.

"A dark force is stirring, threatening our planet's safety, and I need to join your parents to encounter it."

Lina's eyes wandered across the rolling hills, her heart heavy with the weight of her family's secrets. She felt like a leaf, torn from its branch, drifting aimlessly on the wind.

"Aunt Ameera, why must you leave?" Lina asked, feeling upset that another family member must leave.

Aunt Ameera's expression turned grave, her eyes clouded with concern.

"Your parents need me, Lina. The crisis on Ananke demands my attention. I must help them navigate the treacherous waters of intergalactic politics. Noctora's threats have not deescalated yet."

Dina's face crumpled, tears welling up in her eyes.

"But what about us? Where will we go?"

Aunt Ameera's smile was a gentle, warm breeze on a summer's day.

"Lina, I will be able to secure a place for you at Safa Grammar School, a prestigious boarding school. You will be safe there and receive an excellent education. You will make new friends and discover new talents."

Lina's heart sank like a stone dropped into a bottomless well.

"And what about me?" Dina asked, her voice trembling.

Aunt Ameera's eyes softened as her head tilted to one side. "You will stay with Mrs Habib, a trusted friend. She will care for you like her own and nurture your creativity. "

"But I want to be with Lina," Dina pleaded.

"I know, but they don't have space for both of you, my dear," said Aunt Ameera reassuringly. "But don't worry, you will be close to each other. You can call each other every evening and visit Lina on the weekends."

"Okay," said Dina hesitantly, looking at the floor.

****

Lina's stomach twisted into knots as she packed

her bags, her mind racing with doubts. What if she didn't make friends? What if the classes were too hard? What if she could not cope without Aunt Ameera and Dina? She felt like a bird about to be pushed out of its nest, forced to fly before she was ready.

"Aunt Ameera, I don't want to go," Lina said, her voice trembling as she hugged her aunt tightly.

Aunt Ameera stroked her hair, her voice soft.

"I know, dear one. But you'll grow and learn so much at Safa Grammar School. "

Dina clung to Lina, tears streaming down her face.

"I will miss you so much, Lina! Who will I share my secrets with?

Lina's eyes welled up with tears as she hugged Dina.

"You will always have Mrs Habib, and we'll talk to each other all the time. We will share our secrets. "

"But it's not the same," Dina whispered, her voice cracking.

"We'll always be connected, no matter where we are. Our bond is unbreakable, remember," Lina said with affection.

Dina nodded a small smile on her face.

"You are right. We'll always be together in spirit."

5

BOARDING SCHOOL

It was the day before the new school term started. School boarders had to arrive at their boarding houses by 6 p.m., giving the students enough time to unpack, relax, and have everything in order for the first day of school.

Aunt Ameera offloaded Lina's bag by the school

gates and gave Lina a long, loving hug.

"You will have a wonderful time," reassured Aunt Ameera.

"Yeah sis, call me when you're next free," insisted Dina, after giving Lina a tight hug.

Lina wanted their conversation to continue forever, but they all knew they had to depart—at least for the time being.

Aunt Ameera and Dina slowly entered the car and departed the school grounds. Lina bid farewell and watched the car drive away until it was out of sight.

Now, alone, her heart was heavy with uncertainty. She felt a void, like a star extinguished in the night sky. As she turned around, she took a deep breath.

"You can do this Lina. Nothing is difficult for you. Just inhale and focus on your breathing," she whispers to herself repeatedly.

As Lina stepped into the grand atrium of Safa Grammar School, a spectrum of emotions swirled within her. The sudden departure of Aunt Ameera and Dina - like a shooting star vanishing into the cosmos, had left her feeling alone.

With each step, her footsteps echoed through the halls, a rhythmic declaration of her presence, like a drumbeat summoning the courage within. The whispers of fellow students she would soon meet fluttered through the corridors. A gentle breeze rustled the leaves, carrying words of welcome and intrigue.

As she entered her dormitory, a warm tapestry of colours and textures enveloped her, like a haven of comfort and belonging. Lina's heart, a flame flickering with uncertainty, began to burn brighter, casting a golden light upon the faces of her new companions.

At this moment, Lina knew she had found a new orbit, a place where her dreams could revolve around the axis of knowledge and friendship. Her entry at Safa Grammar School was a cosmic event, heralding a journey of discovery and growth.

"Hello, dear! My name is Mrs Humphrey, and I'm the house mistress here at Willbrook House. I'll be looking after you and the other girls in this dormitory."

Lina smiled and extended her hand.

"Nice to meet you, Mrs Humphrey. My name is Lina."

Mrs Humphrey shook Lina's hand warmly. "Welcome, Lina! We're delighted to have you join our community. I'll show you to your room and help you settle in."

As they walked to the room, Mrs Humphrey chatted with Lina, making her feel at ease. Once they arrived, Mrs Humphrey smiled warmly as she welcomed Lina into her new dorm room.

"I'm so glad you're here, Lina! You're going to love it at Safa Grammar School."

Lina's eyes widened as she took in her new surroundings. Her new bedroom was large and contained two of everything for her and her new roommate, whenever that would be. Two single beds were on either side of the room, followed by a single wardrobe, a chest of drawers and a shelf on the wall. All the furniture was wooden, the walls were beige, and the carpet was grey. The large windows overlooked the vast grounds that the school was built on. It was all so simple, but it was plenty for Lina.

"Thank you, Mrs Humphrey. It's all so new."

Mrs Humphrey chuckled.

"I know it can feel overwhelming initially, but don't worry, you'll settle in quickly. This school has a way of making everyone feel at home."

Lina nodded, feeling a sense of wonder.

"I can see that. It's so beautiful here."

Mrs Humphrey nodded as she sat on the edge of one of the desks.

"Yes, it is. And it's not just the buildings and grounds that make it special - it's the people too. We have a wonderful community here, and I know you'll fit right in."

Lina smiled, feeling a sense of belonging already.

"Thank you, Mrs. Humphrey. That means a lot to me."

"That's what I'm here for, dear. Now, I should let you know that you don't have a roommate yet, as the room-share rota was created after you joined the school. But not to worry, things change termly."

Lina nodded, curious as to who her future roommate would be.

"Okay, thank you for letting me know."

Mrs Humphrey stood up.

"I'll let you get some rest now. But don't hesitate to come to me if you need anything, okay?"

"Yes, thank you," Lina said.

*****

While Lina navigated the halls of Safa Grammar School, Dina settled into her new life with Mrs Habib, Aunt Ameera's trusted friend. Mrs Habib had a cosy little house with a garden full of flowers. As the days passed, Dina grew closer to Mrs Habib. She shared stories of her parents and Lina, her eyes sparkling with memories of their adventures on Ananke. But despite the comfort and security of her new life, she missed Lina, her best friend.

At night, she would gaze up at the stars, her heart reaching out to Lina, wherever she was. She felt an inexplicable connection to her sister as if their bond was a thread that stretched across the vast expanse of space. And she closed her eyes, Dina could swear she heard Lina's voice, whispering secrets and stories of their shared past, reminding her that even in separation, their connection remained unbroken.

Secrets of Lina's Necklace

6

LINA'S FIRST DAY

The following morning, Lina woke up naturally from a combination of nerves and excitement. She didn't need Ananke's suns on her face. Instead, she was focused on what would come on her first day.

Safa Grammar School rose before her, its stone façade a testament to tradition and learning. The sprawling campus, with its manicured lawns and ancient trees, seemed a world away from the vibrant planet of Ananke. Lina's footsteps slowly moved through the corridors, her heart pounding. Her first day at Safa Grammar School was a whirlwind of new experiences and emotions.

As she entered the school corridor, a chorus of curious glances greeted her. Her unique features and necklace drew attention, leading to whispers among the students.

"Who's that girl with the weird necklace?" someone whispered.

"I don't know, but she looks so different," another student replied.

Lina's heart sank, feeling like an outsider. She could see other girls looking at her up and down as if they were trying to figure her out. Mrs Humphrey said the students were special and that the school was a wonderful community for all. It didn't exude that energy at all.

As Lina walked into the classroom, her eyes scanned the room, taking in unfamiliar faces. Some smiled at her, some were expressionless, and some stared like they hadn't seen a girl like Lina before, which was true, as I doubt they had ever met a girl from Ananke before.

She glanced around the desks and saw a girl sitting by the window, her hair shining in the sunlight. Her eyes, a deep shade of brown, sparkled with curiosity as she took in Lina's unique necklace and striking features. A gentle smile spread across her face, inviting Lina to approach.

Feeling a sense of trepidation, Lina hesitated momentarily before making her way to her desk. As she sat down, the girl turned to her.

"Hi, I'm Eve," she said, her voice warm and friendly, "I'm new here."

Lina felt a bit calmer as she took in Eve's kind expression.

"Hello, I'm Lina. I'm new as well," she replied in a calm, low tone. Lina saw the warmth in Eve's eyes, the gentle curve of her smile, and felt an instant sense of belonging.

"Nice to meet you, Lina. Are you looking forward

to math class?" Eve asks.

"I think so. I don't know what to expect," she said whilst flicking through her workbook.

Just then, Mrs Rose walks in.

"Morning, girls, and welcome to the new girls in the class. I hope you had a lovely summer break. Now let's get started with class. Did anyone go anywhere exciting this summer?

A girl put her hand up immediately.

"Yes, you," pointing at the girl. "Please stand up, introduce yourself and tell us where you went."

"Hello, everyone. My name is Tasneen, and I recently visited Rome, Italy. Well, to be exact, I was on a fruit farm in a small town in Montopoli di Sabina, an hour's drive from Rome." She babbled, keen to share lots of information about herself.

"Wow, sounds beautiful. And how far is this place from London?" asks Mrs Rose.

"Urm, I'm not sure. Maybe 1000 metres from here or 1500 metres?" Tasneen said, unsure.

"1000 metres? Are you sure? So if I take one large step, which is roughly 1 metre, you're telling me 1000 steps I'll be in sunny Rome?" said Mrs Rose inquisitively.

Tasneen corrects herself, "Oops, I mean miles?"

Mrs Rose smiles.

"Well done, that's more like it. You see, girls, Math is everywhere in our daily lives, shaping the world around us. Geometry plays a key role in designing and constructing buildings, roads, dams, and bridges. It's also found in nature—consider the hexagons of a beehive, which fit together perfectly to maximize space efficiently. Measurement helps us explore and understand our surroundings, whether calculating the distance to the sun or determining the height of a tree. Through data analysis, we uncover patterns and trends in the environment, deepening our understanding of the world we live in."

Mrs Rose was strict and expected the girls to know a lot. The class continued for 50 minutes, and Lina felt overwhelmed by the amount of information she has to take in during her first class. Additionally, it was only 10 a.m., and she still had another 6 hours until school finished for the day.

The loud sound of the school bell rang to end the class, and the girls packed their books away. Lina was used to having classes outdoors, under the sun, where the sun shone brightly all day long. Her classes in Ananke were different. Each lesson had regular breaks to appreciate the nature that surrounded them. Being on Earth felt different and fast-paced in comparison. This was an experience she would have to get used to quickly.

"How did you find your first class?" Eve asks.

"Not bad. I think, but I already feel tired," Lina giggled.

"Don't worry. There are just a few more classes, and we have lunch break followed by PE. Before you know it, your first day will be finished, and you can get some rest," Eve reassures her.

"By the way, I love your necklace. Where did you get it?" Eve asked.

Lina's smile faltered and then bloomed. "Thanks! My family gifted me it."

Eve's eyes widened. "That's so cool! It's very pretty. I heard people whispering about it in the corridor earlier. Try to ignore people's comments if you can," Eve said with a slight smile.

"Thanks," replied Lina. She looked down, and as she went to zip up her school bag, she gazed at Eve's bracelet and felt a surge of emotions. The intricate patterns and colours seemed to speak to her, evoking memories of her home planet.

"It's beautiful," Lina said in her gentle voice. The colours reminded her of her planet's sunsets.

Eve smiled, her eyes sparkling.

"I'm glad you like it. My parents got it for me before they left. They live abroad." She went to pull her jumper over her bracelet, feeling shy.

Lina's heart swelled with empathy.

"I know how hard it is to be away from family. But your bracelet, it's like a piece of home, isn't it?"

Eve nodded, her expression understanding.

"Exactly. It makes me feel closer to them, even when apart." Lina's fingers instinctively went to her necklace, a symbol of her connection to her parents and home planet.

"I feel the same way about my necklace," Lina

said, her voice filled with emotions.

"It's like a bridge between my old life and my new one."

Eve looked at Lina with compassion.

"We may be far from our loved ones, but we have each other now. And these reminders of home keep us connected. "

Lina nodded to agree. They picked up their bags and walked out of the classroom together.

7

SCHOOL LIFE

As the weeks went by, Lina and Eve became good friends. They explored the different parts of the school together and discovered hidden corners, secret gardens, and even an old, mysterious-looking tree that was hollow inside.

Lina walked down the hallway, her necklace

gleaming in the fluorescent light. Mila, flanked by her friends, sneered at her.

"Hey, weirdo, what's with the ugly necklace?" Mila taunted.

(Mila, the queen bee of Safa Grammar School, revelled in her popularity and influence. With a sharp tongue and quick wit, she effortlessly manipulated those around her, bending them to her will. Her piercing blue eyes seemed to bore into those she targeted, making them squirm under her gaze.)

Lina's eyes narrowed.

"It's none of your business."

Mila snickered.

"Oh, I think it's everyone's business. Rumour has it, that thing's worth a fortune."

Lina's face remained calm, but her mind raced with comebacks.

"You don't know anything about it," Lina replied, her voice steady.

Mila's friend June snickered, egging her on.

"Oh, come on, Lina, share the secret."

Lina's patience wore thin.

"I said it's none of your business."

Mila's smile twisted.

"Fine, be that way. But mark my words, we'll find out what makes that necklace so special. "

As the weeks went by, Mila's bullying escalated, targeting Lina in different places around the school. In the canteen, Mila snickered loudly, pointing at Lina's necklace.

"Hey, look at Lina's fancy jewellery! Must be nice to be so rich."

Lina's eyes flashed, but she remained calm, taking a bite of her sandwich.

"At least I don't have to rely on spreading rumours to feel important."

Mila's face reddened, but Lina just smiled sweetly and continued eating.

Mila blocked Lina's path in the hallway, flanked by her friends.

"You think you are so special with that necklace, don't you?"

Lina stood tall, her eyes locked on Mila's.

"I'm special because I'm me, not because of some

object. You should try being confident without putting others down. "

Mila sneered, but Lina's words struck a chord, and for a moment, Mila's mask slipped, revealing a glimmer of insecurity.

In history class, Mila whispered loudly,

"What's with her clothes? She dresses so differently. "

Lina's gaze turned icy.

"What are you going to do about it?"

The teacher intervened, but Lina's response had already made an impact. Mila's friends exchanged uneasy glances, and for the first time, they saw Lina as a force to be reckoned with.

Despite the bullying, Lina continued to shine, her confidence and inner strength inspiring others. She walked down the hallway, her head held high and her necklace gleaming like a badge of honour.

"You know, Lina," Eve said as they walked together,

"you're awesome. You never let them get to you."

Lina smiled.

"I've learned to rise above, my dear!"

As the bell rang, signalling the end of the school day, Lina felt a sense of relief wash over her. She had navigated yet another day of Mila's bullying with grace and confidence. Lina headed to her dorm room, the soft glow of the setting sun casting a warm light on her path. She climbed the stairs, her footsteps quiet on the carpeted floor and pushed open the door to her cosy room.

Lina settled onto her bed, phone in hand, and dialled Dina's number.

"Hey Dina! How's life with Mrs Habib?"

Dina's cheerful voice replied,

"Hey, Lina! Life is great! I love my home-schooling schedule with Mrs Habib. I learn on the computer and help her with her garden and chickens."

Lina chuckled.

"That sounds amazing! I'm stuck here dealing with bullies like Mila. She's been making fun of my necklace, saying it's too fancy and I think I'm rich."

Dina's tone turned sympathetic.

"Aww, sorry to hear that. That's so mean of her. What do you say to her when she said those things?"

Lina's voice filled with confidence.

"I just tell her I'm special because of who I am, not because of some object. And I remind her that she should try being confident without putting others down."

Dina's voice filled with admiration.

"You're so brave, Lina. I don't know if I could handle that."

Lina smiled.

"It's not easy, but I won't let her get to me. I'm going to keep being me. I don't have time for bullies."

Dina laughed.

"That's the spirit! And hey, at least you have Eve to support you. What's she like?"

Lina's eyes lit up.

"Eve is great! She's so kind and supportive. We have so much fun together."

"That's nice. I'm happy for you sis. I'm learning about gardening and animal care. Did you know Mrs Habib's chickens can produce different coloured eggs?" Dina said. She was keen to share what she's learned.

Lina laughed.

"No way! That's so cool. I wish I could see them."

Dina's voice filled with excitement.

"You will! Just wait for the end of term. We will show you around the garden and introduce you to the chickens." Lina smiled.

"I'd love that. And then we can give the chickens names."

Both girls chatted for a while longer, enjoying each other's company and sharing stories about their lives.

****

Later that night, when Lina was sleeping, her phone rang, breaking the silence of her room. She hesitated momentarily, thinking Mila had gotten hold of her number to bother her again, before realising that it was her parents calling to check in.

"Hey, Sweetie! How's school going?" her mother

asked, her voice warm and comforting.

Lina sighed, feeling a mixture of emotions.

"Hi, Mum," she yawns. "It's okay, but it's also been tough. There's this girl, Mila, and she's been bullying me along with her friends. "

Her father's voice turned serious.

"Bullying? What's going on?"

Lina explained the situation, leaving out no details. Her parents listened attentively, their concern growing with each passing moment.

"Lina, we're so proud of you for standing up for yourself," her father said.

"Remember, their words don't define you. You are strong, capable, and loved. Bullies never win in life, remember that. You're a winner, so always remain calm and controlled during conversations with her. She doesn't know you, so for her to make comments is just silly. It's because you are a new girl, so she needs something new to target. Try to ignore it as best you can." Her father went on passionately.

"Don't lower yourself to her level," her mother added from the background.

Lina's heart swelled with gratitude.

"Thanks Mum and Dad. I feel better now. "

"And don't let Mila and her friends get a hold of your necklace. This is very important Sweetie, do you understand?" Her father said in a more serious tone.

Lina smiled, feeling a sense of responsibility wash over her.

"Yes Dad, I promise, it's safe with me."

"Okay, darling, sleep well and speak soon. We love you very much," her parents said before hanging up.

Her parents' reassurance and trust gave Lina the courage to face Mila and her friends once again. She knew she wasn't alone and that her parents and sister would always be there to support her. With renewed determination, Lina ended the call, ready to face whatever challenges lay ahead.

The rest of the winter term flew by in a blur. Lina worked hard, enjoying her classes and spending time with her friends while ignoring Mila's comments.

As the term drew to a close, Mr Johnson reminded them,

"Don't forget, you have homework to complete

over the break. And don't miss out on the new classes next term — they'll be out of this world!"

Lina grinned, excited about the adventures to come. She left the classroom happy and content, with a sense of wonder and anticipation for the next term.

8

REMINISCING

It was the end of the term, and Lina was thrilled to see Mrs Habib and Dina walking towards her at school.

"Lina, dear, how are you?" Mrs Habib asked, giving her a warm hug.

"I'm doing great, Mrs Habib! Thanks for letting me stay with you this break," Lina replied, beaming.

"My home is your home, Lina," said Mrs Habib.

Dina grinned.

"We want to know everything about school. So, tell us, what's new?"

Lina's eyes sparkled.

"I've made some amazing friends. And I've learned so much about Earth customs, like 'afternoon tea'. I drink a cup of tea while eating something called a scone. It's rather lovely.

Mrs Habib smiled.

"That's wonderful, Lina! You're really enjoying the new culture."

The next few weeks were spent at Mrs Habib's house. Lina got to meet the chickens and the vegetable patch. The three of them spent the evenings getting to know one another.

"What's been your favourite experience so far in England?" Mrs Habib asked the girls.

Lina thought for a moment.

"I think it was trying all the new foods in Central London. And learning about the different holidays and traditions here."

Mrs Habib nodded.

"Food is a big part of any culture. I'm glad you're enjoying it."

Mrs Habib asked,

"And how are your classes going? Are you enjoying your studies?"

Lina nodded enthusiastically.

"Yes, I am! My favourite subject is science, and my teacher, Mr Johnson, is great. He makes the lessons so much fun."

Dina smiled.

"That's terrific! We're glad to hear that you're enjoying your classes."

Lina added,

"And I've also been learning about Earth, space, and science. It's fascinating to see how different it is from Ananke's."

Mrs Habib nodded.

Dina asked,

"Have you tried any new sports or activities?"

Lina grinned mischievously.

"Actually, I tried out for the school netball team,

and I made it! It's been a lot of fun playing with my new teammates."

Mrs Habib beamed with pride.

"That's wonderful, Lina!"

Lina smiled, feeling happy and content.

"Thanks, guys. I'm just trying to make the most of my time here on Earth."

"As you should. Which reminds me. Aunt Ameera told me you girls should be taken out to try a different cuisine this holiday? What do you say? I'm thinking Asian food!" Asked Mrs Habib, keen to get moving.

"That sounds like a great idea, Mrs Habib!"

Lina and Dina nodded enthusiastically.

"Great, let's get going then," said Mrs Habib, getting up from the armchair.

*****

They got into the car and made their way to their local town centre. The sun set early during the winter days, and all the street lights were turned on, creating a warm, golden glow that lined the roads. The lights reflected off car windows and puddles, adding a magical charm to the journey and making the road feel inviting and alive.

The three of them stepped into the cozy Pakistani restaurant, greeted by the aroma of freshly baked naan and sizzling kebabs wafting from the kitchen. The warm lighting reflected off intricately carved wooden decor and framed traditional art, creating a homely atmosphere. As they settled into their seats and opened the menu, they were met with a list of flavorful dishes they didn't quite recognize. The girls looked at each other hesitantly.

"What's all this?" asked Lina.

Mrs Habib smiled.

"We'll try something new today. How about a biryani?"

Lina and Dina exchanged a hesitant glance, but Mrs Habib reassured them,

"Trust me, you'll love it."

When the biryani arrived, they took a bite. Their eyes suddenly widened in surprise.

"Wow, this is spicy!" Exclaimed Lina.

Dina started coughing.

"Water. We need water!" She said, now with a husky voice, pushing her words out.

In a panic, they grabbed a stranger's drink from the next table and gulped it down. The stranger looked shocked, and Mrs Habib rushed over to apologise.

"Mrs Habib, help!" Lina almost cried, still coughing.

Mrs Habib quickly grabbed a pot of yoghurt and forced a spoon into each of their mouths.

"Keep the yoghurt in your mouth to cool it down. It may take a minute. And please, never take someone else's drink without asking. That's not only rude but also unhygienic!"

Dina's face turned bright red.

"We didn't know what to do. It was so spicy!"

Mrs Habib smiled patiently.

"I know, but there are better ways to handle it. Let's try to be more mindful, okay?"

Lina nodded while eating a big pot of yoghurt. "We're sorry, Mrs Habib. We didn't mean to be rude.

The stranger, who had been watching the

commotion, smiled kindly.

"No worries, I'm just glad I could help. Maybe next time, ask for a milder dish, okay?"

Mrs Habib thanked the stranger and turned to the girls.

"Let's order something else, shall we?"

Dina and Lina nodded, still embarrassed but grateful for Mrs Habib assistant.

After surviving a meal spicier than they'd anticipated, Lina and Dina leaned back in their chairs, faces flushed and eyes watering, but laughing uncontrollably.

"Who knew biryani could be so dramatic?" Lina gasped, fanning her mouth with a napkin. Dina, clutching her pot of yogurt, took generous gulps, having ditched water in favor of this ultimate spice antidote. They couldn't stop laughing as they relived the chaos—especially Dina's blunder of calling *naan* "flatbread pancakes." As they strolled out of the restaurant, tears of laughter in their eyes, Lina declared with a grin,

"Next time, we're bringing a fire extinguisher!"

*****

With only a few days left of the school holidays, Mrs. Habib decided it was the perfect time for a picnic in the park—despite the chilly grip of winter.

Bundled in layers, Lina and Dina trudged along, carrying a basket packed with sandwiches, fruit, and thermoses of hot chocolate.

"Don't worry," Mrs. Habib chuckled as they laid out the blanket on a frosty patch of grass.

"No biryani today—I wouldn't want another *spicy drama*!" Lina burst out laughing, while Dina muttered,

"I wouldn't mind some flatbread pancakes, though," earning a playful nudge from her sister.

They sat huddled together for an hour or two, sipping hot chocolate and marvelling at the frozen pond nearby.

"Alright, girls, finish up. We need to head home soon. Tomorrow, Lina, we're off to buy whatever you need for the new school term. Pencils, notebooks... maybe a fire extinguisher?" Mrs Habib teased with a wink. Lina groaned but couldn't help smiling.

As they walked back the the car, Lina turned to Mrs Habib and Dina with a smile.

"Thank you both. I had an amazing time this holiday."

Mrs Habib smiled back.

"You girls are like a part of my family. I'm here for you both if you need anything."

*****

The evening before Lina had to leave for school, the girls sat in the garden, watching the stars twinkle to life, Dina turned to Lina with a curious expression.

"Do you think Mum and Dad are okay?"

Lina hesitated, unsure of what to say. But as she looked up at the stars, she felt a strange connection to the universe, a sense of hope and resilience.

"I'm sure they are, Dina. We'll hear from them soon. "

"I'll miss you when you return to school," Dina said, feeling a little sad.

"Me too, but remember, you can call me whenever you want. I'll always make time for you," replied Lina.

"Funny, how in Ananke we never say things like 'I miss you'. I usually say things like, 'Get away from me! I hate you!" Said Dina, chuckling.

Lina chuckles back. "That's so true, but it's just us two now, so we've got to stick together."

The girls rested a little longer before heading to bed. Lina felt a little sad knowing she would return to school the following evening, but she was also excited about seeing her friends again.

****

It was a chilly Sunday evening in January, and the boarding school buzzed with life as students returned from the holidays, dragging suitcases and calling out to familiar faces. Lina sat at her desk in her quiet dorm room, the hum of voices and footsteps filtering in through the small gap under her door. The sun had already disappeared below the horizon, leaving the frosty grounds bathed in the pale glow of the school lights. Lina was hunched over her workbook, finishing her last-minute homework. The radiators hummed as they were on full blast to help keep the cold at bay. The distant sound of laughter and rolling luggage was interrupted by a firm knock at the door, jolting her. She froze for a moment, then glanced up. "I wonder who that could be?" she mumbled, pushing her chair back.

Just then, the girl burst into the dorm room with a bright smile.

"Hey, I'm your new roommate, Jennie!

Lina smiled back, slightly startled.

"Hey, I am Lina."

"I finally have a roommate, how exciting!" Lina said to herself.

Jennie dropped her bags on the floor and began to unpack.

"So, Lina, how's it going? I hope I'm not interrupting anything. "

"Wow! Jenny speaks really fast," Lina thought
    to herself.

"She also unpacks really fast as well", she says, giggling a little.

Lina shook her head, wanting to appear friendly.

"No, not at all. Just studying, you know, last-minute homework and all."

Jennie nodded, having already unpacked everything from her bags.

"Cool. I'm glad we're roomies now. I've heard great things about you. "

Lina raised an eyebrow, unsure what to make of Jennie's enthusiasm.

"I mean, Mrs Humphrey, the Housemistress, tells me you are super neat, super organised, and super clean. She also said you are super respectful to teachers, which is awesome and super cool. No wonder all the teachers like you," said Jennie.

The speed of her words reminded Lina of her journey from Ananke to Earth – it was super fast!

"The teachers like me?" Lina thought to herself.

"Well, that's good," she said, smiling, feeling rather chuffed and proud of herself. She then visualised herself on a podium with a medal around her neck with the words engraved 'Best Student on Earth'. Okay, that was a little exaggerated. Maybe it should say 'Best Student on Earth (followed by her younger sister Dina).' After all, she loved Dina to bits, so it only seemed fitting to have her on her medal as well. Or maybe that would also make Dina want the medal since it had her name on it. Okay, maybe 'Best student on Earth, followed by her younger sister' was perfect because it mentions Dina without actually saying her name so that she wouldn't want it. Maybe all that extra writing would mean they have to engrave my name really small to fit that all in. Perhaps there could be two medals, one each, with mine saying 'Best Student on Earth' and Dina's saying 'Best student standing next to me'. And she could only wear that medal while standing next to me, so it could remind her of what a fantastic person and great student her sister is.

"Hello, Lina? Earth to Lina. Are you with us?" said Jennie, waving her hands in front of Lina's face.

Lina was light-years away with the stars, thinking about her medal.

"By the way, Mrs Humphrey's asked me to tell you that Mr Satori needs you to rewrite the English essay you emailed during the holidays. Something about you not doing it right. Sorry, I forgot the message, I had a lot of things going through my head at the time," said Jennie.

"Maybe she was planning where to unpack everything as she unpacked in record lightning speed," Lina said to herself.

"No problem. I'll ask Mrs Humphreys. Thanks for telling me," she said, smiling. But then she stopped smiling as she realised that maybe she wasn't the 'Best Student on Earth' after all if she was getting her homework all wrong.

"Never mind," she whispered to herself.

9

A NEW TERM

The new term began with a flurry of activity as students bustled through the school corridors, their voices filling the air with stories of winter break adventures. The once-quiet halls now hummed with energy, the lively chatter echoing off the walls as friends reunited and shared their holiday tales. Mr.

Johnson, the science teacher, stood at the front of the room with a warm smile.

"Good morning, everyone! Welcome back to school. I hope you all had a wonderful break and are ready to dive back into your studies."

The class murmured a collective "good morning" as they sat at their desks. Lina sat next to Aya today as Eve was at the school nurse's office feeling unwell.

Mr Johnson continued,

"I know you're all eager to start, so let's get right into it. We have a lot to cover this term, and I'm excited to see what you all will accomplish. This term, I'll be introducing some new classes, including cosmology and astronomy. You'll even use the school telescopes to explore the night sky!"

Lina's heart skipped a beat. This was exactly what she had been waiting for. She couldn't wait to learn more about the stars and planets.

After class, Jennie headed over to Lina.

"Hey, Lina! Mrs Humphrey asked if you could show me around today since I'm new here."

Lina smiled and nodded.

"Of course, I'd be happy to help. We've got sports class next, so let me show you where the sports hall is."

As they walked to the hall, Lina and Jennie were getting to know one another. Jennie chatted excitedly about her holidays, and Lina listened intently.

When they arrived at the sports hall, their teacher, Mr Brooks, greeted them.

"Welcome, everyone! Today we're going to play hockey.

As they played, Lina couldn't help but notice Mila and her friend Jade snickering on the sidelines. She tried to ignore them and focus on the game, but when Mila commented on her necklace, Lina felt her patience wear thin.

"Don't worry about my necklace, thanks. Just focus on your own faults," she said, brushing past Mila.

Jennie looked at her in confusion.

"What's going on?" she whispered to Lina.

Lina just shook her head.

"Don't worry about it. Let's just focus on the game."

Despite the drama, Lina and Jennie had a great time in sports class, and she was glad she could help Jennie feel more comfortable. As they left the gym, Jennie thanked her for her help.

"No problem," said Lina, smiling.

10

SOMETHING GOES MISSING

The following morning, Lina prepared for school with her usual care, checking her packed bag and straightening her uniform. But as she reached into her drawer for her necklace, a jolt of panic shot through her. It was gone. Frantically, she tore through the drawer, patting every corner, sifting through her clothes, and searching again and again. Each frantic motion deepened her dread — her necklace was nowhere to be found.

Panic set in as she thought about the importance of the necklace. Without it, she felt exposed and vulnerable.

"Ok Lina, stay calm and think! You got this," she told herself.

Lina's eyes narrowed as she thought about Jennie, her roommate. She had been acting suspiciously friendly, and Lina could not shake off the feeling that Jennie might be involved in the necklace's disappearance.

"Why would she take it?" Lina thought to herself. "Why would she want it? She is a new girl after all."

Lina's eyes scanned Jennie's belongings, searching for any sign of the necklace. But as she rummaged through Jennie's bags, she realized that Jennie didn't have it. She put everything back neatly so Jennie wouldn't suspect anything as she returned from her morning shower.

Feeling a little dizzy from confusion, Lina quickly

grabbed her phone and went to the boarding house's sitting room to call her parents.

Lina's hands trembled as she held the phone to her ear.

"Mum, Dad, I lost the necklace. I can't find it in my room, I don't know what to do," she blurted out as her voice was now matching the speed of Jennie's.

Her mother's voice was firm.

"Are you sure Lina? We need you to find it urgently. "

Lina felt a pang of worry.

"I know, I'm sorry. I'll do everything I can to find it. "

Her Father's voice came on the line, his tone polite but stern.

"Lina, we're counting on you. We know you are responsible and capable. We need you to search every inch of your room and school and talk to anyone who might have seen it. "

Lina took a deep breath.

"Yes, you can count on me. I'll find the necklace," she said, a bit calmer.

The phone call ended, and Lina knew she would find the necklace no matter what it took.

During lunch break, she decided to confide in Eve, her closest friend.

"Eve, I need to talk to you about something," Lina said, pulling Eve into a quiet corner.

"What's up?" Eve asked, noticing Lina's worried expression.

"My necklace is gone," Lina said, trying to keep her voice down.

"I thought maybe Jennie, my roommate, took it, but I searched her stuff, and she doesn't have it."

"What made you think it was her that took the necklace?" asked Eve

"She was always really friendly, and it made me suspicious of her, but I went through her belongings, and it wasn't anywhere."

"That's weird. Why would someone steal it? That's so out of order!"

Lina nodded,

"I know. But I have a bad feeling about this. The necklace is really important for me and my family. "

Eve's eyes sparkled with an idea.

"Lina, I think I know who might have taken your necklace." They both looked at each other.

"MILA," they said at the same time quietly. Lina nodded, her mind racing.

Eve leaned in.

"You reminded me that I overheard Mila and her friends talking about a 'weird trinket' they found. I didn't think much of it at that time, but now I am wondering if it was your necklace. "

Lina's eyes widened as the pieces fell into place.

"I saw her eyeing my necklace before."

Eve nodded.

"I knew it! Mila's always been a bit shady. We need to confront her and get your necklace back. "

Lina felt a surge of determination.

"Let's do it. I'm not going to let her get away with this. "

Together, Lina and Eve hatched a plan to confront Mila and retrieve the necklace.

*****

The school cafeteria was buzzing with chatter and laughter as students caught up with each other during their lunch break. The aroma of freshly baked pizza and sandwiches wafted through the air, mingling with the sound of clinking utensils and plates. Groups of friends clustered together, sharing stories and jokes, while others sat alone.

Lina and Eve approached Mila's table. Lina clenched her hands into fists, her determination evident on her face.

"Mila, we need to talk," Lina said, her voice firm but controlled.

Mila looked up, a hint of surprise on her face.

"What's up, Lina?" she replied, barely making eye contact as if she was uninterested in speaking with her.

Lina's eyes locked onto Mila's. "I know you took my necklace. I want it back. "

Mila's expression changed from surprise to innocence.

"I don't know what you are talking about."

Lina's gaze narrowed.

"Don't lie to me, Mila. That's my necklace. "

Mila's eyes darted around the cafeteria, her nervousness evident, "I ..... I don't know what you're talking about. "

Eve stepped forward, her voice firm.

"Mila, we're not playing games. Return the necklace, or we're going to the head teacher. "

Mila's face paled, but she maintained her innocence.

"I don't have your necklace. You're just paranoid."

Lina's frustration grew. She knew Mila was lying, but she could not prove it yet.

Lina walked off with Eve following. Feeling deflated and frustrated, Lina leaned up against the corridor lockers and took a deep breath.

"Now what?" said Eve.

"Of course, she would deny taking it. How can she admit it with everyone there? We need to figure out what she wants the necklace for."

Lina's face was downcast, and her ears rang as she

felt numb. Everything seemed to have slowed down. She looked at the floor, noticing the texture of the thin carpet, the colour of the classroom doors, and the brightly coloured notice boards hung up along the corridor filled with students' work. Other students walked aimlessly towards their upcoming classes, laughing at each other. All Lina could hear was white noise at that moment; she felt disconnected from reality.

Her parents relied on her to keep the necklace safe. There was so much pressure to look after it, and what for? She needed some answers.

"Leave it for now," said Lina, struggling to push the words out of her mouth. She walked to her next class, knowing she needed to speak with Aunt Ameera later that evening.

11

THE NEXT MOVE

That evening, Lina went into the storage room in her boarding house—a private area where people barely went. It was filled with boxes, each containing all sorts of items that the boarding house would need. She pulled out her phone and dialled Aunt Ameera's number, her fingers moving quickly over the keypad. She waited momentarily, listening to the ringtone before Aunt Ameera's warm voice answered.

"Hi Lina, so lovely to hear from you," Aunt Ameera said.

"Hi, Aunt Ameera. I need to talk to you about my necklace," Lina said, getting straight to the point.

"Ah, yes. The necklace. What's going on, dear?"

"Mila, a girl at school, took it. She denied it, but I know she has it. I feel so lost and frustrated," Lina explained.

"Mum and Dad seemed very concerned that it's lost, and I don't know what to do."

Aunt Ameera's tone turned serious.

"Lina, your necklace is special, that's why. It's not like any other. It has a unique power - one that can protect Ananke if needed."

"Really? What do you mean? And why my necklace and not someone else's necklace?" Lina asked, curiosity piqued.

"Each necklace is unique, each with its own strength. Yours is particularly precious, Lina. The centre stone is rare because it is unbreakable, and its power can help shield Ananke from harm." Aunt

Ameera revealed.

"You need to find it," Aunt Ameera added. "Do whatever it takes to get it back, Lina. I know you can do it!"

The call ended with Lina knowing it was up to her to find her necklace again. She would find her necklace, no matter what it took.

With newfound determination, Lina decided to keep a low profile and avoid Mila until she came up with a plan to retrieve her necklace.

****

One weekend, Lina and Eve sat in Lina's room, brainstorming their next move.

"We need to get into Mila's room and search for the necklace," Lina said, her determination evident.

Eve nodded,

"But how? We can't just barge in."

Lina thought for a moment.

"I've got it. We'll wait until Mila goes for lunch and then sneak into her room. "

Eve's eyes widened.

"That's risky. What if we get caught? Her boarding house is another building, so it will look obvious going in and out of it. Mrs Handford, the house mistress, will know we don't sleep there and won't let us upstairs."

Lina's jaw clenched.

"We'll be careful. We'll make sure no one sees us. We can wait for Mrs Handford to go for lunch as well, and that's when we quickly head upstairs. "

Eve nodded, a plan forming in her mind.

"Okay, let's do it, but we need to be really quick and quiet."

They hatched a plan, deciding to sneak into Mila's room during her lunch break. They would search every inch of the room, leaving no stone unturned.

****

The bell rang for lunchtime, and they knew they

had to work fast. They waited outside her boarding house until Mrs. Handford left for lunch.

"There she goes," whispers Lina.

"Ready?" Lina asked as they stood. Eve nodded.

Lina took a deep breath. They quickly ran upstairs, then slowly turned her door handle and pushed open the door. They slipped inside, scanning the room for any sign of the necklace.

Lina and Eve searched every inch of the room, but there was no sign of the necklace. They looked in every drawer, under the bed, and even in the closet. But it was nowhere to be found.

Lina's frustration grew with every passing minute. She had been so sure that Mila had the necklace, but now it seemed she had been wrong.

"Where could it be?" Lina muttered aloud.

Eve shook her head.

"I don't know. But we'll find it. Let's keep looking."

But Lina was done looking. She was tired of searching, tired of hoping, and tired of being disappointed.

"This is so ridiculous," Lina said, her voice rising.

"I know Mila took it. Why can't we find it?"

Eve tried to calm her down, but Lina was beyond reason. She was consumed by frustration and anger.

"I don't care where she hid it," Lina said, her voice trembling.

"I just want it back!"

Eve put a hand on Lina's shoulder, but Lina shook her head and walked away, feeling demoralized.

They left her room quickly and exited the building, grateful that everyone was at lunch so they weren't spotted.

12

ANOTHER STRATEGY

Lina sat on her bed, feeling defeated. She had been searching for her necklace everywhere, but it was nowhere to be found. Eve approached her.

"I've been thinking, Lina. What if Mila didn't take the necklace for herself but gave it to someone else to hide it for her?"

Lina raised an eyebrow.

"Who would she give it to?"

Eve said,

"June. She is Mila's closest friend. Maybe Mila gave the necklace to June to hold onto so that she would not be suspected."

Lina's mind raced as she considered Eve's words. It was possible. Mila and June were inseparable. And if Mila wanted to throw them off her trail, giving the necklace to June was the perfect move.

With another plan hatched, Lina set out to uncover the truth. Their next stop was June's room, where they hoped to find the missing necklace. The only problem was that everyone had finished their lunch and was heading back to their boarding houses to relax before classes started again.

"We don't have time to search her room now," Eve said.

"What if she moves the necklace before we get a chance to find it? What if Mila notices we moved her things? We already confronted her, so maybe she's more cautious and checking what we're up to." Lina said nervously.

"That's doubtful. We were very careful when moving her things and ensuring they were all returned correctly. And no one saw us enter and leave her boarding house. Don't worry about it. We'll just have to wait until tomorrow to try again," Eve suggested.

Lina was distracted for the rest of the day, swinging her pencil back and forth like a seesaw against her geography book.

"What's the answer, Lina?" Mrs Anderson asked. "It looks like the answer is written on the wall with the way you're staring at it," she continued.

Lina wasn't focusing and felt too upset about her necklace being taken. She felt sad that she had broken her promise to her parents, telling them she would keep it safe. This made her feel sick in the stomach.

"Sorry, Mrs Anderson. What was the question? I'm feeling a little unwell today." Lina said, downcast.

"Do you want to go to the nurse's office?" asked Mrs Anderson.

Lina didn't know how to reply. On one hand, she

wasn't concentrating in class, but it kept her busy. And on the other hand, if she went to the nurse's office, she would be spinning the same thoughts and questions around in her head.

"I don't know. Can you decide for me, please?" Lina said glumly.

The class chuckled amongst themselves. They've never heard that reply before.

Mrs Anderson smirked.

"Ok, girls, let's try a new exercise. Everyone stand up, and let's move the tables and chairs to one side."

Lina liked knowing they were doing something active to distract her. It was just what she needed to help her get through the day. Now was not the time to overthink things. It was class time, and Lina enjoyed Geography. She enjoyed learning about planet Earth. There were so many places she wanted to visit and explore.

Mrs Anderson handed out small flags and stickers to each student.

"Today, we're going to play a game called 'Country Quest.' Each of you will represent a country, and you'll need to stick that country's flag on your back. Then, your classmates will ask you yes or no questions to guess which country you are."

Lina's flag was Japan, and she carefully stuck it to her back.

The game began, and students started asking questions.

"Are you in Europe?" "Do you speak English as an official language?" "What's a typical dish that represents your country?"

Lina answered the questions about Japan, trying to give subtle hints without giving away the answer. Meanwhile, she was trying to guess which country Eve was.

"Are you a member of the European Union?" she asked.

Eve nodded, and Lina thought,

"Ah, that narrows it down a bit."

As the game continued, Lina found herself having fun despite her earlier worries about her necklace. She liked learning about different countries and cultures, and this game was a fun way to do it.

After a few minutes, Mrs Anderson called out, "Time's up! Now, take a guess at which country you think each of your classmates is?"

Lina looked at Eve and took a guess.

"I think you're France!" Eve smiled and nodded.

After the geography exercise, Lina headed to her sports class, feeling a bit more energized. As she walked towards where her classmates were, she saw Mila standing by the tennis courts, racket in hand. Lina's competitive streak kicked in - she wanted to beat Mila at tennis.

Lina had an advantage. Back in Ananke, she played a sport called 'Sky Ball', which involved hitting a ball with a racket while floating in mid-air. The hand-eye coordination and timing she developed playing Sky Ball would be useful on the tennis court. Especially as tennis was a much easier game to play.

The instructor paired Lina and Mila up against each other, and the match began. Lina focused on her game, using her Sky ball skills to anticipate Mila's shots and hit precise returns.

Meanwhile, on the sidelines, Aya watched the

match while munching on a chocolate bar from the UAE.

"Hey, Lina, you're doing great!" she called out.

"By the way, I have some amazing chocolate flavours from back home - rosewater, cardamom, and orange blossom. You should try them sometime!"

Lina smiled and nodded, distracted from the match for a moment.

"Yeah, that sounds delicious! I'd love to try them later."

But for now, she was focused on beating Mila. She served an ace, and Mila returned it with a weak shot. Lina pounced on the opportunity and hit a winner, taking the point.

Mila scowled, but Lina just smiled sweetly. She was determined to win this match.

The match intensified, with both Lina and Mila playing their best shots. But Lina's Sky ball training gave her an edge. She anticipated Mila's moves, using her agility and quick reflexes to hit precise returns.

As the game neared its end, Lina was ahead 40-15. Mila tried to make a comeback, but Lina was relentless. She hit a powerful forehand winner, and Mila couldn't return it.

The instructor called out,

"Game, set, and match! Lina wins!"

Lina felt a rush of triumph as she shook hands with Mila. She had beaten her rival and proved her skills on the tennis court.

As she walked off the court, Aya congratulated her with a warm smile.

"You were amazing out there! I knew you'd win. Now, about those chocolates."

Lina laughed, feeling a sense of camaraderie with her friend.

"Definitely, Aya. I'd love to try them. But first, let's get some water. I'm parched after that match!"

Together, they walked off the court, talking about chocolate, of course.

*****

The evening sun cast a warm orange glow over the boarding house as Lina made her way to the shower. She let the warm water wash away the sweat and stress of the day, feeling her muscles relax.

After dressing in comfortable pyjamas, she headed to the sitting room, where some friends were gathered around a table.

"Hey, Lina! Come join us for some card games," called out Jo.

Lina smiled and sat down, shuffling the deck. They played a few rounds, chatting and laughing together. The group of friends talked about their favourite foods and holidays.

After a while, Lina excused herself, feeling tired.

"I'm going to bed, guys. See you tomorrow!"

*****

The following day, Lina woke up feeling refreshed. She walked alongside Eve to the dining hall in the main school building for breakfast.

"Today's the day!" Lina whispered, her eyes

sparkling.

"We're going to search June's room during lunch."

Eve nodded.

For now, Lina set her worries aside and focused on the morning's activity—a school-wide scavenger hunt. Teams of students raced around the campus, solving clues and collecting points in a spirited competition. This beloved school tradition, dating back over a hundred years, awarded the winning team a coveted trophy displayed proudly in their boarding house. It was a reminder to all students that with focus and determination, anything can be achieved.

Teams were made up based on the boarding house you were from, so Lina's team included Eve, Jennie, Jo and a few other girls from different year groups. They worked together seamlessly, using their problem-solving skills to overcome obstacles. They laughed and joked as they ran from one clue to the next, enjoying the sunny day and each other's company.

Lina's boarding house was a lively mix of girls from diverse backgrounds. Most evenings, they gathered to chat, play card games, and share snacks, fostering a strong bond of unity and cooperation. This companionship proved invaluable during the scavenger hunt, enabling them to work together seamlessly, solve clues quickly, and ultimately win the competition with ease.

The girls erupted into laughter, sharing a massive group hug as the rest of the school cheered—well, most of them. A few, including Mila and her friends, stood off to the side, less enthusiastic.

Unbothered, Lina's joy remained intact. When their housemistress, Mrs. Humphrey, proudly held up the large trophy adorned with hanging tassels, the girls cheered wildly, forming a circle and jumping up and down in celebration.

As the morning drew to a close, Lina felt carefree and happy. She had almost forgotten about the necklace and the mystery surrounding it. But as she walked into her class before lunch break began, she spotted June sitting at a table, looking smug. Lina's determination returned, and she knew that today was the day she would search June's room.

The school lunch bell rang, and Lina quickly went to Eve's classroom.

"Quickly," she whispered to Eve.

"This is our only chance for today."

They casually walked over to June's boarding house, trying not to look suspicious, and waited for Mrs Handford to go to lunch. They waited for five minutes, but she wasn't leaving the house.

"What do you think she is doing in there? Maybe she left for lunch earlier?" said Eve, thinking aloud.

"Maybe, but we don't have forever to wait. We need to enter, and if she is there, we need a backup plan quickly," said Lina.

"But we need to think about what we are going to say because I don't want to lie," said Eve nervously.

"Agreed. There is never any benefit in lying, however, maybe we can go see Aya afterwards, as she's always receiving new chocolates from her family abroad. That's not lying," replied Lina.

"Good point," said Eve.

"Ok, let's just go," said Lina without overthinking about what was to come.

They walked in casually, looking around in the foyer.

"Mrs Handford, are you here?" asked Lina calmly.

No answer.

"I don't think she is here," Lina said quietly but excitedly.

They calmly walked around the corner towards the stairs.

"What are you girls up to?" said Mrs Handford from inside the laundry room.

The girls froze. It was time for one of them to say something casually and not lie.

"Oh, hello, Mrs Handford. We called for you in the foyer but didn't get an answer, so we thought it was ok to head on up," said Lina quickly.

"I didn't hear with the washing machine on, dear. Who are you here to see?" Mrs Handford inquired.

"We came by to see Aya. She recently received chocolates from a family member in the UAE," said Lina confidently.

"How lovely, I've been there, and it's beautiful. They certainly have lovely chocolates over there. If you ever go there, visit Patchi. Each chocolate is individually wrapped. They are lovely with some tea."

Mrs Handford was going into a lot of detail, and although the girls didn't mind, it was shortening their time to search June's room.

"We were just going to quickly check if Aya has popped in now," said Lina, trying to rush things along.

"Yes, dear. I'm not sure, but her room is in the other direction, down the south wing," said Mrs Handford, pointing in the other direction.

"Thank you," the girls said, walking that way.

The other direction? The other side of the house? Luckily for the girls, there was a long corridor upstairs that connected the wings together; however, navigating the longer way around was riskier, as rushing around was wasting time, and they didn't want to be seen in another wing that they weren't meant to be in.

"Let's be quick, Eve," said Lina. "I don't want to be sent to the head teacher's office."

They hurried upstairs, making sure no fire door slammed as they made their way through the corridors.

They finally found June's room. Her door was already open.

Lina turned to Eve.

"Is she in there?" she said, moving her lips but not saying anything so no one would hear her.

Eve stopped moving and held her breath to make sure she could just hear silence. She then shook her head.

They walked inside cautiously, looking behind the door to ensure no one was in the room.

"Let's do this quickly," said Lina, rushing nervously.

They searched every nook and cranny but despite their thorough efforts, the necklace remained elusive, nowhere to be found. Lina's frustration grew with each passing moment, her hope of recovery dwindling.

"Nothing! There is nothing here! Let's just go," Lina said quickly but frustrated.

They walked back the way they came in, retracing all their footsteps until they got downstairs.

As they were leaving the house, Mila and June walked past them. They barely looked at each other. No smile was in sight.

Mila looked over her shoulder as she saw the girls run off. She then saw Mrs Handford.

"What were Lina and Eve doing, Mrs Handford? They were too much in a rush to tell me," said Mila, feeling smug.

"They came to visit Aya. Something about some sweets they were going to have." Replied Mrs Handford.

Mila's eyes skewed. She had just seen Aya in the dining hall having lunch with her friends. Mila knew Lina was up to something.

*****

The day continued with Lina enjoying her classes. Her mind was numb, and she didn't want to think much about anything else.

As Lina walked out of her last class, she met up with her friend Sophia, who was also on the badminton team. They walked towards the sports hall together to get ready for the after-school team practice.

"Hey, Lina! How's it going?" Sophia asked.

"It's going ok," Lina replied.

"I'm just glad the day is over. I'm so tired."

"Yeah, I know what you mean," Sophia said.

"But hey, at least we have badminton practice to look forward to!"

Lina groaned.

"I don't know how you enjoy playing with those rackets. It's so much harder than using a tennis racket!"

Sophia laughed.

"That's what makes it fun! And you're actually really good at it. You're one of the best on the team."

Lina smiled, feeling a bit proud.

"Thanks, Sophia. I guess it's just something I've gotten used to."

Just then, Lina's phone rang. She answered it, and her sister, Dina, was on the other end.

"Hey, Lina! How's school?" Dina asked.

"It's ok, I guess," Lina replied.

"Just tired. How about you? How's your cooking classes going?"

Dina laughed.

"It's going great! I made the best chicken parmesan yesterday. But I have to tell you, I tried to make fish and chips today, and it was gross!"

Lina giggled.

"Well, at least you're trying new things! I'm proud of you. But wait, where did you get the chicken from? Please tell me you didn't eat Mr.Sushi, my favourite chicken?"

Dina laughed out loud.

"No, no! I chose Mr Plump. He looked rather plump, so I thought he was the best choice."

"Phew. Ok, glad you enjoyed your meal sis. Please take care of Mr. Sushi and Mrs. Fluffball. No eating them until I'm back, ok?" Said Lina with a smile in her voice.

The two sisters chatted for a bit longer before Lina's badminton practice started. She hung up the phone and headed into the sports hall, feeling a bit more energized after talking to her sister.

*****

As the evening sun dipped below the horizon, Lina stepped into the shower, letting the warm water wash away any negativity she felt. She had been searching for her necklace for what felt like an eternity, and the frustration was starting to take its toll. As she ran a brush through her damp hair, she realized she needed a hair clip to hold up her locks. Her own clip had snapped earlier, and she had been teased mercilessly by her classmates for having messy hair - not that she cared.

Lina padded over to Eve's room, hoping to borrow a clip. Eve lived in a separate room just across the hall from Lina's. Lina knocked softly on the door, and when there was no answer, she assumed Eve was out or asleep. She slowly turned the handle and slipped inside. The room was dimly lit, with only a sliver of moonlight illuminating the space. Lina made her way to Eve's dresser, thinking she wouldn't mind as they were such good friends, hoping to find a hairclip.

As she opened the drawer, she noticed something strange - a faint glow emanating from beneath the clothes. Curiosity piqued, Lina pushed aside the garments and found the source of light - her necklace. It lay nestled in the corner of the drawer, radiating a soft, ethereal glow.

13

A PHONE CALL WITH FAMILY

Lina's heart skipped a beat as she stared at the familiar pendant. She felt a mix of emotions: shock, confusion, and hurt. Why was her necklace in Eve's drawer? Had Eve been hiding it from her all along? Did Mila know we went through her room and place it in Eve's room so I would turn against my friend?

Lina's mind raced as she tried to process this new information. She thought about all the times Eve had offered to help her search for her necklace, all the times Eve had seemed so concerned about her loss. Had it all been a ruse, a clever act to distract Lina from the truth?

With trembling hands, Lina carefully placed the clothes back in the drawer, making sure to leave everything exactly as she had found it. She didn't want Eve to suspect that she had discovered the truth. Not yet, at least.

As she slipped back into her own room, Lina could not shake off the feeling of betrayal. She felt like she had been punched in the gut, her trust shattered into a million pieces. She didn't know what to say or what to do, so she said nothing, pretending that everything was normal. But deep down, Lina knew that nothing would ever be the same again. The friendship she thought she had with Eve was possibly a lie, a facade hiding a darker truth.

Before taking action, Lina thought it would be wise to calm down first. A clear mind made her react more appropriately so she would know exactly what to say.

Firstly, she called her sister Dina, seeking her advice and guidance, knowing that Dina would be her rock in this challenging situation. She knew that Dina's calm and level-headedness would help her find the best way to retrieve her necklace and deal with Eve's betrayal. With a deep breath, Lina dialled Dina's number.

"Hey Lina," Dina's voice was warm and comforting over the line.

"Hey, Dina! I need to talk to you about something," Lina said, her voice trembling.

"What's up? You sound upset. " Dina said, her tone immediately concerned.

Lina took a deep breath.

"I found my necklace," she said in a sad tone.

"I'm guessing by your tone, it wasn't Mila, was it? And why are you not a little excited that you have it back in your possession?" Said Dina

"I didn't take it because it's in Eve's drawer! Eve, my best friend," Lina said in a loud whisper.

Dina's voice was laced with worry.

"Eve? Oh no, Lina. She's your friend. I can't think that she can do something like this. "

"I know, me neither. That's why I'm so shocked," Lina said, feeling sad.

"This is not good, Lina. Why would Eve want to steal it from you?" Dina asked, her voice filled with concern.

"I don't know, Dina. I feel so confused about it all." Lina said, feeling a sense of vulnerability.

"Maybe it was planted there?" Dina said, trying to make numerous excuses for Eve.

"That was the first thing I thought, but then again, what if it WAS her that took it? I need to speak with her," said Lina anxiously.

"Don't worry, Lina. We'll get it back. But you need to be careful. You can't let Eve know that we know she took it," Dina advised.

"And Lina, be careful around Eve from now on. We don't know what she's capable of," Dina warned.

"Okay... I will try," Lina said.

"I'm here for you. We'll get through this together. If you want to confront her, I want to be there. Two is greater than one, after all," Dina said, smiling, her voice filled with reassurance.

"That's great math skill, Dina. Well done," she said sarcastically.

"But that's a good idea, I want you there with me as well. Let's speak with her this weekend."

"Sounds good, sis. I can't wait to see you." Said Lina excitedly.

"In the meantime, I'll just have to remain calm and see it through a few more days until you're here," said Lina.

"Yeah, sis, don't worry, we'll get your necklace back soon," said Dina.

"Thanks, sis. Good night."

"Good night."

Lina put her phone down and lay on the bed, her mind replaying the conversation with Dina. Dina's words echoed in her mind: "We'll get through this together."

Lina's eyes drifted to the clock on her nightstand.

Her eyes were heavy as she fell asleep.

*****

The following day, Lina walked into school as if it were any other morning. She entered her classroom, and as she sat down, her teacher walked over to her.

"You are called to the head teacher's office, Lina. You need to go there immediately."

"I'm being called to see the head teacher? Me? What could this be about? Maybe Mila found out I was in her room," she muttered to herself.

Many questions raced through her mind, and her stomach filled with butterflies as she walked towards Mr Hunt's office.

As she approached his office, his assistant told her to take a seat. Lina turned around and saw Mila and June sitting there with their arms crossed and legs folded, trying to look intimidating. But Lina didn't care about their immaturity. This experience made her miss her parents and Ananke even more.

As they waited to be called in, Lina glanced at the

girls whispering between themselves. Mila took out a ring. It was really pretty, covered in lovely green and white stones.

"Wait a minute! Was that the shiny trinket that Eve had mentioned? Maybe that was it and not my necklace. So it had nothing to do with Mila after all." Lina said to herself. Her eyes fixated on the ring.

"Where did you get that ring from, Mila?" Lina asked.

Mila paused before responding.

"I found it in the park. Why do you care? Are you going to take it from me to match your necklace?" Mila replied, with June sniggering beside her.

"But that's not yours then. Someone is out there looking for it. If I find something lost, I leave it there in clear sight so people can retrace their footsteps and find it easily. Or return it to the person in charge of that area. And no, I don't want it. It is pretty though."

"Finders keepers, lemon sheepers," said Mila, playing with her new ring.

"I think you'll find its 'finders keepers, losers weepers,'" Lina corrected her.

"Whatever," Mila said dismissively, not interested in further conversation.

The fact that the ring was indeed a shiny trinket just proved that it was Eve who took the necklace. But why?

Mr Hunt came out of his office and stood tall over the girls.

"Right, girls, I've heard from multiple sources that you girls are not getting along. We don't tolerate bullying here. Everyone has their differences, but we must learn to live in harmony with one another." He paused.

"Now, I wanted to hear the full story from both sides to resolve the matter once and for all, but I have a faculty meeting now, so we will postpone it until further notice. Until then, learn to accept your differences and move forward with your lives."

He locked his door and walked off. "Excuse me, sir, your window is a tiny bit open, but you locked your door," Lina said.

"Yes, I do that to get a constant small draft into my office. There is nothing better than returning to the nice smell of fresh air in my office. Right, off you girls go to class. Learning awaits," he said sternly, ushering them off.

Lina, Mila, and June walked in the same direction down the corridor toward their class.

"I heard you lost your necklace. That sucks. It was really pretty. I would totally keep it if I found it in the park," Mila said, smiling a bit.

"Thanks. I know it's out there somewhere," Lina smiled back.

A heavy energy was lifted, and Lina didn't feel so hostile towards Mila anymore. She couldn't be bothered to retaliate with snide remarks. Her focus was more on Eve now and getting back what was hers.

14

TIME TO GET IT BACK

Lina couldn't wait until the weekend to confront Eve. She wanted her necklace back, and she wanted to do it now! Delaying it to the weekend could give Eve time to move it, and it would be lost forever.

Lina needed to wait for the perfect moment to retrieve her necklace from Eve's room. She thought about Eve's schedule, trying to remember when she was usually busy or out of her room.

As she waited, Lina's thoughts turned to her friendship with Eve. Had she missed any signs? Had Eve been struggling with something, or was this just a betrayal? Lina's mind was swirled with questions, but she pushed them aside, focusing on the task at hand.

When it was quiet, Lina snuck quietly into Eve's room. She slowly opened the drawer to retrieve her necklace. She was now inches from finally being reunited with her necklace again.

Lina's eyes widened in shock as she gazed into Eve's drawer, the space where the necklace once lay, now an empty space. Her heart sank, and her mind raced with the terrible thought that the necklace was gone forever. Panic set in, her breath catching in her throat as she frantically searched the room, hoping against hope that it had simply been moved elsewhere in the room.

Lina's hands trembled as she closed the drawer, her eyes fixed on the empty space where the necklace once lay. She felt a wave of despair wash over her, the weight of her loss settling heavy on her shoulders. The necklace was more than just a piece of jewellery; it was her responsibility to keep it safe, a promise she made to her parents that would help protect Ananke. Everyone is at risk now.

Lina's mind was a whirlwind of thoughts, each one more unsettling than the last. Eve's actions had set off a chain reaction of anxiety and confusion within her. Why did Eve take the necklace? What did she plan to do with it? The questions swirled in Lina's mind like a vortex, pulling her down into a sea of uncertainty.

As she tried to make sense of Eve's motives, Lina's anxiety grew. She couldn't shake the feeling that Eve was hiding something, that there was more to her actions than met the eye. The thought sent a shiver down Lina's spine, her heart racing with anticipation.

But what could Eve possibly want with the necklace? Lina wondered. Was she looking to sell it? The thought seemed absurd, but Lina couldn't shake it off. Maybe Eve saw the necklace as a way to make a quick profit, unaware of its true significance.

Lina's confusion deepened as she tried to

understand Eve's perspective. Why would she want the necklace if she didn't know its importance? The question seemed to defy logic, yet Lina couldn't shake the feeling that Eve was driven by something more than mere curiosity.

Lina's hands trembled as she dialled Dina's number.

"Dina, it's Lina. I need to talk to you about something," she said, trying to keep her voice steady.

"What's wrong, Lina?" Dina asked, concern etched in her voice.

"The necklace is missing again. I went to Eve's drawer, and it's gone," Lina replied, her words tumbling out in a rush.

"Have you checked her room thoroughly?" Dina asked, her voice firm.

"I mean, every inch of it?"

"Yes, I've checked everywhere," Lina replied.

"I've looked under the bed, in her closet, even in her desk drawers. It's nowhere to be found."

"Are you sure?" Dina pressed.

"Maybe you missed something. A hidden

compartment or something?"

"I'm positive, Dina," Lina said.

"I've checked everything. I even moved her furniture around to see if it was hidden behind something. "

There was a pause on the other end of the line before Dina spoke up.

"What are you going to do now? What can I do to help?"

"We need to find out more about Eve," Lina replied.

"How are we going to do that?" asked Lina.

"We don't even know where to start."

"I do! But I will need your help." Said Lina.

15

ANOTHER BREAK IN

The girls greeted each other with a tight hug. Lina saw Dina's cute necklace hang softly around her neck. It wasn't the same as hers. Dina's was more subtle and had smaller stones than Lina's, which had an orange-coloured rounder pendant in the middle.

"You see that office over there?" Lina said, pointing.

"That's Mr Hunt's office, the head teacher. It's where he keeps all the student records. If we search Eve's records, I'm sure we can find out more about her. Let's sneak in and see if we can find anything in her file."

"Are you sure, Lina? You could get into a lot of trouble," Dina pleaded.

"I need answers, sis. Mum and Dad are counting on me. They might need it soon, so I want to be prepared to show them," Lina replied.

Dina nodded.

"Okay, sis." She had nothing else to add, as she wasn't keen on the idea, but she wanted to help her sister.

Lina walked over to the office and slowly turned the handle.

"Great! It's locked!" Lina said.

"I should have known that. I even saw Mr Hunt lock it on his way to a school faculty meeting. Of course, he'll lock it on a weekend. What was I thinking?" She exclaimed, with her palms on her forehead.

"WAIT! I know! I remember he left his window open ever so slightly and said he enjoys the constant breeze entering his office. HIS WINDOW! We must enter through his window. I know he hasn't locked it."

They walked quickly around the back of the building to where the window was.

"Which window is it? There are quite a few," Dina said.

Lina scanned the windows from a distance and noticed one slightly raised.

"That one!" They ran over. The window was higher up than they thought.

"You'll have to hoist me up, Dina. Clasp your hands together, and I'll stand on them to raise myself up."

Lina and Dina reached the window.

"Okay, I'm ready," Lina said, placing her foot in Dina's clasped hands.

Dina heaved Lina up, and with a bit of effort, Lina managed to push the window open and wiggle through. With her arms out front, she landed softly and wriggled her legs through the window until she stood upright again.

"Made it!" Lina whispered triumphantly.

"Now, let me help me get you in."

Dina looked up at the window, then at Lina.

"Just don't drop me, okay?"

Lina grinned.

"I promise I won't."

Dina carefully climbed into Lina's hands, using her feet to climb up the wall outside until she eventually climbed through the window. Once Dina was inside, she brushed off her clothes and looked around.

"This place smells nice," Dina said, inhaling deeply.

"I guess Mr Hunt really does enjoy the fresh air. It's like walking into a breezy garden."

Lina chuckled.

"Yeah, I can almost imagine him standing here, taking in the air like he's on vacation. Alright, let's be quick and get out of here before we make any noise."

As they moved around the office, they both enjoyed the unexpected freshness of the room. The gentle breeze from the open window added a touch of calm to their covert operation.

Dina looked at Lina, smiling.

"You know, for a mission that started a bit stressful, this isn't so bad. We should get caught breaking into offices more often if it means enjoying this kind of fresh air."

Lina laughed quietly.

"True. It's like a breath of fresh air—literally. Let's just make sure we don't overstay our welcome."

Dina nodded.

"Definitely. We'll find what we need and get out before this becomes a full-blown adventure."

They shared a brief, amused glance before focusing on their task. The light-hearted moment helped ease the tension, making their secretive mission a little more enjoyable.

They were together in the office, their hearts pounding in unison. They made their way to the cabinet where student records were kept, their fingers flying as they searched for Eve's folder.

"its here!" Said Lina in a loud whisper.

As they opened the folder, Lina's eyes widened in

surprise.

"She has no relatives in the country," she whispered, her brow furrowed in confusion.

Dina's eyes scanned the paperwork, her expression equally perplexed.

"And look at this - a large down payment to ensure her daughter got a place in the school." But as they delved deeper into the paperwork, their excitement turned to disappointment. There were no clues, no hints, and no leads. It was as if Eve's past was a blank slate.

Lina lay her head on the cabinet, feeling defeated.

"There's nothing here!" I need to go tell Mum and Dad that the necklace is lost for good," she said with little energy left in her.

But Dina didn't give up. She scanned the paperwork again, her eyes scanning every detail.

And then, she saw it - a small signature, easily missed, but with letters that seemed to match their home planet of Ananke.

"Lina! Come look at this, the letters are so familiar."

Lina's eyes locked onto the signature, her heart racing.

"I recognize these letters. They are so similar to Ananke. Where is Eve from?"

Just then, a flashback rushed through Lina's mind. She remembered Eve's bracelet from the first day they met. Lina had complimented it, but Eve had quickly covered it with her top. Lina had thought Eve was just shy, but now she realized that Eve didn't want them to know the truth about who she was. The stones on the bracelet were the same ones used on their home planet.

"What does she want with my necklace then?" Lina wondered aloud.

They turned to each other.

"She must be from Noctora," Dina said. "That would explain the large down payment to secure her place in the school. She must have wanted to get close to me to befriend me and steal my necklace. She'll use it against Ananke."

"We need to get that necklace back immediately!" Lina said urgently.

Without a word, the sisters decided to confront Eve, determined to get to the bottom of the mystery.

16

TIME FOR THE TRUTH

The next day, Lina and Dina stood before Eve, their eyes blazing.

"Tell us the truth, Eve," Lina demanded.

"What's going on? Why did you take my necklace?"

Eve's smile was enigmatic, her eyes glinting with secrets.

"You want to know about the necklace?" she asked, her voice low and husky.

"Yes, we do," Dina replied, her voice firm.

"What's so special about it?"

Eve's laughter was coarse, sending shivers down Lina's spine.

"The necklace is just a small part of a much larger plan," she said, her eyes glinting with excitement.

"What plan?" Lina asked, her curiosity piqued.

Eve's smile grew wider, her lips curling up in a cruel smile.

"My planet, Noctora, has been seeking to conquer Ananke for centuries," she revealed, her voice dripping with malice.

"And the necklace is the key to our victory."

Dina's eyes widened in shock.

"What do you mean?"

Eve's eyes gleamed with excitement.

"The rare stone in your necklace is crucial for Noctora's plans to breach Ananke's defences and launch an invasion."

Lina's face paled, her heart racing with fear.

"You can't be serious," she whispered.

Eve nodded, her expression unyielding.

"I'm completely serious. My parents, who are part of Noctora's ruling council, sent me to Earth to steal and bring the necklace back to them."

Dina's voice was steady, her words laced with conviction.

"We'll never let that happen. We'll stop you and your planet's evil plans."

Eve's laughter was like a cold wind.

"You're no match for Noctora's power," she sneered.

"We have the technology and resources. All we needed was your necklace. The rare stone at its centre, once hidden deep within the darkest caves, was excavated and lost—vanishing without a trace. That is, until someone reported back to Noctora having seen it on a girl's necklace. That girl was you, Lina. You have no idea of its power, but now it belongs to Noctora."

The air was thick with tension as the three girls faced off, their destinies entwined in a battle between planets. The fate of Ananke hung in the balance, and Lina and Dina were determined to save it. They just had to figure out where she kept the necklace.

The girl's only choice was to part ways with Eve until they thought of a plan to retrieve her necklace.

Moments later, Lina's phone rang, shrill in the silence. She answered, her heart racing with anticipation.

"Lina, dear, it's Mum," her mother's voice sounded distressed.

"We need to talk about your necklace."

"What about it, Mum?" Lina asked, her brow furrowed in concern.

"We need it back, Lina. Immediately," her mother replied, her voice urgent.

"Aunt Ameera will collect it. We can't delay."

"Why? What's going on?" Lina asked, her curiosity piqued.

"It's the planet's defences, Lina. They're weakening. We need the stone in your necklace to strengthen our shield," her mother explained, her voice laced with worry.

"But why now?" Lina asked, her mind racing with questions.

"Because Noctora's threats are escalating. We

can't afford to be vulnerable. The necklace is our only hope. You see, Lina, it is our job to protect Ananke, and in doing so, we ensured that a precious stone that was gifted to us was kept in our possession. A stone powerful enough to counteract attacks. We concealed that stone within your necklace. When others began mining for these stones, they must have discovered that it had already been excavated. That likely led them to search for its distinct orange hue. A spy must have noticed your necklace and reported it to Noctora, which explains why their threats have only escalated. This is why we need your necklace now," her mother said firmly, her voice unwavering.

Lina's heart sank. She knew she had to tell her parents the truth.

"Mum, I have something to tell you. I tried to get the necklace back from Eve, but I couldn't," Lina said, her voice laced with frustration.

"Lina, who is this Eve you're talking about?" her mother asked, her voice firm.

Lina took a deep breath before revealing the truth. "Eve is from Noctora, Mum. She was sent to steal the necklace, and she stole it! I didn't know until it was too late."

There was a pause on the other end of the line before her mother spoke up.

"Noctora?" her mother asked, her voice laced with worry.

Lina's heart sank as she revealed the truth.

"Eve's parents are part of Noctora's ruling council. They sent her to Earth to steal and bring the necklace back to them. They need the stone to breach our planet's defences and launch an invasion."

There was silence on the phone. Lina's heart raced with anxiety.

"Mum? Are you there?" Lina asked, her voice shaking.

"Yes, I'm here," her mother replied, her voice cold.

"This is unacceptable, Lina."

Lina felt a pang of guilt and regret. She knew she had let her parents down.

"I'll do everything I can to get it back, Mum. I promise," Lina said, determination etched in her voice.

The line went dead. Lina was left staring at her

phone, confusion warring within her. She knew she had to get the necklace back, no matter what it took.

17

CONFRONTATION

Lina and Dina sat together in Lina's room, finalizing their plan.

"Ok, so we'll go to Eve's room and pretend to be scared," Lina said, her voice barely above a whisper.

"And then she'll think she's won," Dina added, her

eyes gleaming with determination.

"Exactly," Lina said. "And then we'll tell her the truth. We'll tell her about Noctora's plans and how she's being used."

Dina nodded.

"And we'll make sure she knows we're not afraid of her."

Lina stood up, her heart pounding with anticipation.

"Let's do this. Let's go confront Eve."

Dina followed Lina out of the room. Their hearts were united in their determination to stop Eve and save their home planet.

They approached Eve's room, their footsteps quiet on the floor. Lina took a deep breath and then opened the door.

Eve looked up from her packing, a sneer on her face.

"Well, well, well. Look what we have here."

Lina and Dina walked in, their eyes fixed on Eve.

"We know what you're doing, Eve," Lina said, her voice firm.

Eve laughed.

"Oh, I'm shaking in my boots."

Dina stepped forward, her eyes blazing.

"We're not afraid of you, Eve. We're here to stop you."

Lina took a step forward.

"We know about Noctora's plans, Eve. We know they're using you to get to our planet's defences."

Eve snorted.

"You're too late. I've already agreed to give them the necklace."

Dina's eyes locked onto Eve's.

"Don't do it, Eve. If you give them the necklace, it will only lead to war and destruction."

Eve shrugged.

"I don't care. I'll do whatever it takes to protect my own planet."

Lina's voice was urgent.

"But that's just it, Eve. You're not protecting your planet. You're helping Noctora destroy ours, and it will only lead to more suffering for everyone."

Eve's expression faltered momentarily, and Lina

saw a glimmer of doubt.

Dina pressed on.

"Think about it, Eve. If Noctora gets the necklace, they'll use it to destroy our planet's defences. But then what? It will start a war, and innocent people will get hurt. And for what? Just for Noctora to rule over more planets? There are no winners, Eve."

Eve's eyes widened as the truth dawned on her.

Lina's voice was gentle.

"We're not your enemies, Eve. We're just trying to protect our home. And we can work together to stop Noctora's plans."

Eve looked at the necklace in her hand and then at Lina and Dina. For a moment, they thought they saw a glimmer of uncertainty.

But then Eve's face hardened.

"Get out of my room," she spat.

Lina and Dina exchanged a disappointed glance, but they knew they had planted a seed of doubt in Eve's mind.

As they left Eve's room, Dina whispered,

"I think we got through to her, Lina. She's thinking

about it."

Lina nodded.

"We'll have to keep trying. We can't give up yet."

*****

The next day, Lina and Dina again crept into Eve's room, their hearts pounding with anticipation. They had to get the necklace before Eve could give it to Noctora. They scanned the room, their eyes locking onto the bed.

And there it was, the necklace, lying on the bed, glinting in the dim light.

Lina's eyes widened.

"It's here," she whispered.

Dina nodded, her eyes fixed on the necklace.

"Let's get it."

They moved forward, their hands reaching out to grab the necklace. But just as they did, Eve appeared out of nowhere, her eyes blazing with fury.

"NO!" she spat, snatching the necklace from the bed.

Lina and Dina tried to grab it from her, but Eve was too quick. She held the necklace aloft, its power surging through her.

And then, the room erupted into chaos. The air shimmered, and a blinding light enveloped them. Lina and Dina stumbled back, their eyes streaming from the intensity of the light.

When their vision cleared, they saw that Eve had created a powerful barrier around herself. The barrier pulsed with a fierce, blue light that seemed to repel everything around it.

Lina and Dina tried to approach but were met with an intense, burning sensation that forced them back.

"What have you done, Eve?" Lina cried, her voice shaking with fear.

Eve's eyes gleamed with triumph.

"I've unlocked the necklace's true power," she spat.

"And with it, I'll protect myself from all of you."

But as she spoke, a dark, shadowy figure began to take shape outside the barrier. It grew larger and larger, filling the room with an unspeakable evil.

Lina and Dina stumbled out of the room, gasping for air. They looked back to see Eve standing in the doorway, the necklace still clutched in her hand. But to their surprise, Eve's expression was no longer one of triumph. Instead, she looked uncertain.

She looked down at the necklace and then back up at Lina and Dina. For a moment, they thought they saw a glimmer of doubt in her eyes.

And then, Eve's hand closed around the necklace, and she whispered a single word -

"Stop."

The barrier around her flickered and died, and the dark energy that had been building in the room dissipated. The necklace's power, it seemed, was no longer active.

Lina and Dina exchanged a wary glance. What was Eve thinking? Had she finally realized the error of her ways?

They took a step forward cautiously.

"Eve?" Lina said, her voice tentative.

"What's going on?"

Eve looked up at them, her eyes searching.

"I. I don't know," she said, her voice barely above a whisper.

"I didn't mean for it to go this far."

Lina and Dina took another step forward, their hearts pounding with hope. Maybe, just maybe, they could still save Eve from herself.

"Eve, it's ok," Lina said softly.

"We're here for you."

Eve looked up at them, her eyes welling up with tears.

"I'm so sorry," she whispered.

"I didn't mean to hurt anyone."

Dina smiled gently.

"We know, Eve. We just want the necklace back, and all this can be over."

Eve nodded a small smile on her face.

"I need time to be by myself," she whispered.

Lina and Dina smiled warmly at Eve.

"It's ok, Eve. We will leave, but this isn't over, ok? We still need the necklace back," Lina said calmly.

Together, they walked away from Eve's room, feeling hopeful and relieved. They knew that their planet was safe and that Eve would make the right decision.

18

AUNT AMEERA
INTERVENES

Aunt Ameera arrived at the boarding school, her expression tense and urgent. She spotted Lina and Dina in the courtyard and hurried over to them.

"Lina, dear, I've come for the necklace," Aunt Ameera said, her voice low and serious.

Lina's heart sank.

"Aunt Ameera, I'm so sorry. I was going to get it from Eve, but—"

Aunt Ameera's eyes narrowed.

"Let's go to Eve's room now. We need that necklace."

The three of them rushed to Eve's room, but when they arrived, Eve was alone, looking smug.

"Where's the necklace, Eve?" Lina demanded.

Eve shrugged.

"My parents took it. They said they were taking it to Noctora as it was needed immediately."

Aunt Ameera's face turned white.

"No. This can't be happening. We have to get it back."

Dina spoke up, her voice laced with concern.

"What does it mean, Aunt Ameera? Why is the necklace so important?"

Aunt Ameera's expression turned grave.

"Lina, Dina, I have to tell you something. Noctora's intentions are far from pure. They want to destroy Ananke, conquer its innocent people, and claim its resources for themselves."

Eve, who had been watching the exchange, snorted.

"That's ridiculous. Noctora would never do that. They just want to be the new ruler of Ananke."

Aunt Ameera's eyes locked onto Eve's.

"You don't know the truth about Noctora, Eve. They're a ruthless empire driven by ambition and greed. They'll stop at nothing to get what they want."

Lina felt a shiver run down her spine.

"What do you mean, Aunt Ameera?"

Aunt Ameera's voice was laced with urgency.

"Noctora has been secretly building a weapon that could destroy Ananke's defences and leave it vulnerable to attack. Now, with the necklace in their possession, they have the key to achieving that."

Dina's eyes widened in horror.

"That's terrible! We have to stop them!"

Aunt Ameera nodded.

"We must get the necklace back and warn Ananke that Noctora now has possession of the necklace."

Eve rolled her eyes.

"You're just trying to scare us. Noctora would never hurt anyone."

Aunt Ameera's gaze turned cold.

"You're wrong, Eve. And soon, you'll see the truth for yourself."

Aunt Ameera left immediately and returned to Ananke alone and empty-handed, her heart heavy with disappointment and worry.

19

A LONE MISSION

The skies above Ananke's capital city darkened as Noctora's fleet descended upon the planet. Laser blasts and explosions rocked the city, sending citizens fleeing for cover.

Ananke's defences were weak, and their strongest weapon - the necklace's power - was gone. The Ananke forces were determined to protect their people, so they rallied their troops for a final stand.

"Noctora will not take our home without a fight!" Safety Council's Head declared, his voice echoing through the city's communication system.

*****

Eve lay in bed, her mind racing with thoughts of Lina and Dina and the necklace's dark power. She had never felt so torn in her life.

As she thought about her friendship with Lina and the trust they had built, Eve's heart swelled with emotion. She couldn't bear the thought of betraying Lina or causing harm to her planet.

But then she thought about Noctora's promises and the future she had been offered. Eve's ambition and desire for control tempted her, making her hesitate.

As the hours passed, Eve's inner conflict only grew stronger. She knew she had to make a decision, but she didn't know what to choose.

Finally, as the sun began to rise, Eve made up her mind.

She knew she had to act fast. Her parents had taken the necklace to Noctora's Tirent Fortress, and she couldn't let them use its power for their own gain. She decided to use the teleporter to Noctora and retrieve the necklace herself.

The teleporter is an advanced piece of technology that helped make Noctora powerful. Eve went into her wardrobe and opened a box containing a teleporting disc. She used the controller to signal it where to land and stood upright on the base plate, which immediately transported her to her destination in Noctora.

Her heart racing with fear. Finally, she made it to where her parents were working. The heavily guarded fortress was surrounded by tight security.

Eve had visited the fortress with her parents a few times, so she was recognised and let in easily.

As she entered the courtyard, she immediately jumped to the third floor, thanks to the country's low gravity. Eventually, she reached the throne room, where her parents sat with the ruler of Noctora.

The necklace lay on a pedestal, its power pulsing through the air. Eve knew she had to act fast.

Without hesitation, Eve grabbed the necklace, to everyone's shock.

"Eve! You're here! What are you doing with that necklace? It's where it needs to be now!" Her mother said, walking over to her to hug her.

"Stay back, everyone! You didn't tell me you were going to hurt innocent people. I don't want to be a part of that plan. I can't let you do this." Shouted Eve, her voice shaking.

"Eve! You were asked to do a job, and you did it perfectly. You should have no concern as to how we proceed from here.

"No! I'll not let you do this. You don't need to rule Ananke. Their people are kind and don't deserve to get hurt.

"Young girl," the ruler said, his eyes skewed and his head bent to one side. "We need more power. I need to rule more and own more.

"You will never be happy, and you will always be

looking for more! Why don't you be happy with what you've got compared to what you don't have!" Said Eve, with a lump in her throat.

"Eve. This is not of your concern. Now pass me the necklace," her father demands.

"STAY BACK!" She shouts.

As her nail scratches the surface of the orange crystal. A force envelops her again, sending heat waves across the room.

A force so strong that everyone in the room hides for cover.

"Please, darling, don't do this," her mother pleads.

"Sorry Mum, but war is not the answer. It must end now!" Replies Eve.

"GET THAT GIRL NOW!" The ruler shouted. "I want that necklace immediately."

"NO!" Her parents shouted as they ran after her, wanting to protect her.

Her parents' high position allowed them to intercom all security guards and tell them not to intervene. The guards liked Eve's parents. They were kind and respectful to them, always smiling and greeting them. This softened the guards' hearts and allowed Eve to run out of the building unharmed.

She quickly headed towards the teleporter hidden in a side road and returned to Earth unharmed. With her heart pounding and beads of sweat trickling down her face, Eve was now back at the boarding school with the necklace clutched in her hand.

She knew she had to return it to Lina and the people of Ananke, who needed its power to defend against Noctora's attacks.

But she knew the journey was far from over. Noctora would stop at nothing to get the necklace back, and Eve was now a target.

Eve rushed into Lina's room, her heart racing with emotion. She barged in through her door. Lina and Dina jumped up in shock from her bed, looking at her with annoyed expressions. Eve took a deep breath and approached them.

"I'm so sorry," Eve said, her voice trembling.

"I was wrong to betray you, Lina. I was trying to prove myself to my parents, to make them proud. But

I didn't realise it would actually hurt people, including you."

Lina's expression softened, and she opened her arms to hug her.

"Eve, it's okay. We know you were manipulated."

"Why are you so forgiving? Especially after what I have done," asked Eve, intrigued.

"Our people don't hold grudges. It's a common practice for our people to forgive others before they sleep that night. It's lighter on our hearts and minds." Replied Lina in her calm tone.

Eve shook her head, holding out the necklace.

"But, it's not okay. I should have seen through Noctora's lies. But I'm trying to make it right now."

Lina's eyes widened as Eve held out the necklace.

"Is that? How did you?" she stammered, her excitement barely contained.

Eve smiled, enjoying the moment.

"I snuck into Noctora's main fortress, made my way to where the ruler was, and retrieved it from under everyone's noses," she said proudly.

Lina's eyes sparkled with amazement.

"That's incredible! I can't believe you risked so much to get it back."

Eve shrugged, downplaying her bravery.

"I had to. I couldn't let Noctora use its power against you and your people."

Lina said, her eyes shining with tears.

"Thank you, Eve. This means everything to me."

Eve smiled, feeling a weight lift off her shoulders.

"Protect Ananke, Lina. Keep it safe from those who would misuse its power."

Lina nodded, her face set to end this once and for all.

"We will, Eve. We promise."

Eve nodded, feeling a sense of peace wash over her.

"I know I can trust you both. You're true friends."

Lina hugged Eve tightly.

"We're glad to have you back, Eve. We're in this together now."

Eve hugged her back, feeling like she had finally found her true place.

"Thank you, Lina."

20

TIME TO FIND PEACE

Lina's hands trembled as she dialled the familiar number on her phone. She had news to share with her parents. News that would change everything.

As the phone rang, Lina's heart beat faster with anticipation. She had been waiting for this moment for what felt like an eternity.

Finally, her mother's warm voice answered.

"Hello, Lina?"

Lina took a deep breath before speaking.

"Mum, Dad, I have something important to tell you."

There was a pause on the other end of the line before her father's voice came on.

"What is it, Lina? You sound serious."

Lina's eyes closed as she gathered her courage.

"The necklace. It's back. Eve returned it to me."

The sigh of relief from her father was audible even over the phone.

"Oh, thank goodness," he said.

But Lina's mother's voice was laced with worry.

"But, Lina, the situation on Ananke is getting serious.

Noctora's forces are closing in, and our defences are weakening."

Lina's grip on the phone tightened. She knew what was coming next.

"What can I do to help?" she asked, her voice

trembling with concern.

Her father's voice was firm.

"We need the necklace, Lina. It's the only way to increase our power and protect Ananke."

Her mother added,

"I'll get Aunt Ameera to come and collect the necklace from you. Just wait for her."

Lina nodded, even though they couldn't see her.

"Okay, I understand. I'll give it to her."

As she hung up the phone, Lina felt a sigh of relief. Her planet was almost safe again.

*****

A few hours later, Aunt Ameera arrived at Lina's school, her expression grave with concern. Lina met her in the lobby, the necklace clutched in her hand.

"Aunt Ameera, is everything alright in Ananke?" Lina asked, her voice trembling.

Aunt Ameera's eyes locked onto the necklace.

"Noctora's forces are........are......" Aunt Ameera could not finish the sentence without tears swelling in her eyes.

"We need the necklace to increase our power and protect Ananke. It's now or never."

Lina nodded, holding out the necklace.

"I know. My parents told me."

Aunt Ameera took the necklace, her hands closing around it like a vice.

"Well, Lina. This means everything to us."

Lina's eyes welled up with tears.

"Please save Ananke, Aunt Ameera. I'm scared for our planet."

"We'll try our best. I'm not sure how much time we have left Lina. Our forces are weakening, and getting your necklace back to Ananke will take a long time.

Eve was listening from around the corner.

"Aunt Ameera. I have an idea," she says, walking towards her.

"Use the teleporter to transport you to Ananke immediately. I will help get you there using my code.

Aunt Ameera's eyes locked onto Eve's.

"That's the best decision you've made today, young girl. You're one of the good ones."

Eve blushed shyly, feeling proud of herself. She showed Aunt Ameera how to use the teleporter, and with that, Aunt Ameera was out of sight. The necklace was finally in her possession, ready to face whatever lay ahead to save Ananke.

*****

Aunt Ameera landed at her destination instantaneously, the necklace in her hand. She made her way to the Security Council's chambers, where the council members awaited her return.

"The necklace," one of the council members breathed as Aunt Ameera placed it on the pedestal.

The room erupted in a flurry of activity as the council members activated the necklace's power. Ananke's defences surged, its weapons charged.

Noctora's forces, who had been on the brink of victory, stumbled backwards as Ananke's defences roared to life.

The Security Council's leader, a wise and aged woman, gazed out at the turning tide of the war.

"With the necklace's power, we will conquer. Noctora will be defeated."

As the council members directed the necklace's energy, Ananke's forces launched a fierce counterattack. Noctora's ships faltered, and their defences were breached.

With that level of power pushed against Noctora, their spacecrafts had no choice but to retreat. Their plans were foiled.

Noctora's leaders realized that Ananke's power, amplified by the necklace, was too great for them to overcome. They knew that continuing the war would only lead to great loss on their side.

In a surprise move, Noctora's leaders contacted Ananke's Security Council, proposing a ceasefire and peace negotiations.

After tense but fruitful discussions, the two sides signed the Treaty of Ananke, a historic agreement establishing a lasting peace between the planets.

The treaty included provisions for mutual defence, trade, and cooperation, ensuring that the civilians of both planets would never again suffer from the war.

21

REFLECTIONS AND GROWTH

As the days passed, Eve, Lina, and Dina found themselves growing closer. Lina and Dina, seeing Eve's transformation, had forgiven her. Together, they spent their last few days of term playing by the lake, sharing secrets, and laughing. They found solace in each other's company, their friendship blossoming like a flower in spring.

Eve, once an outsider, now felt like she belonged. She saw the goodness in Lina and Dina, their kindness and compassion inspiring her to be a better person.

As they walked the halls, Eve felt a sense of pride knowing she had found true friends, friends who accepted her for who she was.

Lina, with her gentle spirit, and Dina, with her fierce loyalty, balanced Eve's fiery passion. Together, they formed a trio, united in their quest for justice and peace.

As they sat together in the courtyard, watching the sunset, Eve turned to her friends with tears in her eyes.

"Thank you," she said in a gentle voice.

"Thank you for accepting me, for being my friend."

Lina smiled, her eyes shining with warmth.

"We're in this together, Eve. Always."

Dina nodded, her face happy.

"We're a team. Nothing can break us."

And in that moment, calmness and peace filled the girls' hearts.

****

That evening, Eve had a knock on her door.

"Come in," she said.

"Eve?" A soft voice calls.

"Mum? Eve ran over for a hug.

"I'm so sorry Mum, I couldn't do it. I couldn't bear to know that my actions meant others would get hurt.

"It's ok darling. When I said get close to Lina to befriend her, I didn't realise you would become best friends and have second thoughts about your mission. I'm proud of you sweetheart," her mother said warmly.

"You're father and I no longer work there. The ruler turned against us when you left with the necklace. It's unsafe for us to be there anymore, so we are moving homes after your term finishes."

"I'm so excited. I can't wait to see where we move to," Eve says excitedly.

They hugged each other tightly. Her mother whispering in her ear.

*****

After a few days, Lina sat on her bed, dialling Aunt Ameera's number. She had been worried sick about the situation on Ananke, and she needed to know what was going on.

As the phone rang, Lina's anxiety grew. What if something had happened to Aunt Ameera? What if the situation was worse than she thought?

Finally, Aunt Ameera's warm voice answered.

"Hello, Lina dear!"

Lina's breath escaped in a sigh of relief.

"Aunt Ameera! I've been so worried about you, Mum and Dad and Ananke. What's going on?"

Aunt Ameera's voice was calm and reassuring.

"Lina, dear, everything is fine. I'm so glad you called."

Lina's grip on the phone tightened.

"Tell me what's happening. Is everyone safe?"

"Dear," Aunt Ameera's warm voice replied.

"The threat to Ananke has been neutralised. Our

planet is safe once again."

Lina sighed in relief, feeling a weight lift off her shoulders.

"Oh, thank goodness!"

"Yes, indeed," Aunt Ameera said.

"And now, it's time for you and Dina to come home, as your summer holidays will start soon. I'll be coming to pick you up when the term ends."

Lina's heart skipped a beat.

"Really? We get to come back to Ananke?"

"Yes, really," Aunt Ameera chuckled.

"You and Dina have been through so much. It's time for you to see Ananke's beauty and experience its wonders yet again."

Lina couldn't wait.

"I'll tell Dina! She'll be so excited!"

"Good," Aunt Ameera said.

"I'll see you both soon. We'll be leaving immediately once you have been collected at the end of term."

Lina hung up the phone, her mind racing with excitement. She couldn't wait to see Ananke. She missed the three suns. She missed the turquoise hills and green trees with brown leaves. She quickly called Dina, sharing the news.

"Oh my God, Dina! We're going to Ananke!"

Dina squealed with delight.

Lina grinned, feeling happy.

Lina and Dina burst with excitement, their laughter and chatter filling the air as they packed their bags for the summer holidays.

"We're finally going back to Ananke!" Lina squealed, her eyes shining with anticipation.

"I know, I can't wait!" Dina replied, her grin matching Lina's. "We're going to have the best summer ever!"

Despite their eagerness and excitement to return, Lina remembered the friends that she had made at her school. She had forgiven Eve, and now she will be leaving her when the summer term ends.

*****

As the term ended, it was time for Lina to say

goodbye to her friends, starting with her roommate Jennie, who packed up her room faster than she unpacked it.

"I'll miss you Jennie, you are one fun roommate."

"So are you. I'll miss the spooky stories we would share with each other at night." Said Jennie.

They both chuckled.

"Bye Aya, thanks for always sharing your yummy sweets from around the globe with me. I loved every moment of it."

"Anytime. I love sharing things. After all, sharing is caring." She said smiling.

The girls all hugged and waved goodbye. As Lina went to collect her bags from inside, she saw Mila exiting her boarding house. As they met each other's eyes, the girls broke out a small smile at each other, indicating that there were no hard feelings. Like Lina's father always told her, 'Bullies never win,' and Mila never won. Instead, she stopped and worked on being a better version of herself, striving to improve and fix her faults.

*****

Just then, the door to Lina's room slid open, and Aunt Ameera swept in, her warm smile and twinkling eyes embracing the sisters.

"My dear girls, are you ready?"

"We were born ready!" Dina replied, giggling.

Aunt Ameera chuckled.

"Excellent! Then let's begin. Our journey to Ananke awaits!"

As they finished packing, Aunt Ameera approached Lina with her necklace that she had given her to protect Ananke.

"Lina, dear, I want you to wear this again," she said, her eyes shining with a deep meaning.

Lina took the necklace, feeling a surge of memories and emotions.

"But Aunt Ameera, I gave this to you to keep Ananke safe."

Aunt Ameera nodded.

"And it has served its purpose well. But now, I want you to wear it to symbolise your connection to

Ananke and your role in its future."

Lina nodded, and Aunt Ameera fastened the necklace around her neck.

"Perfect," she said, stepping back to admire Lina.

As the necklace settled around Lina's neck, it began to emit a gentle, pulsing glow. Lina felt a surge of energy and a sense of clarity wash over her. Suddenly, a vision burst forth in her mind's eye, revealing a glimpse of another challenge ahead.

But instead of fear or doubt, Lina felt a thrill of excitement and anticipation. She saw herself standing strong, facing the challenge head-on, and emerging victorious.

With a sense of determination and courage, Lina thought to herself,

"I am ready for this. I am ready for whatever lies ahead."

Aunt Ameera smiled, seeing the confidence in Lina's eyes.

"You are indeed ready, Lina. The necklace has shown you a glimpse of what's to come, and you have risen to the challenge. You and Dina will face whatever comes next, together and strong."

Lina nodded, feeling purpose within herself. She knew she and Dina would face the future with courage, love, and unity. Bring it on, she thought, I'm ready!

As they were leaving the school grounds, Lina saw Eve talking with what looked like her parents outside a car.

"Eve, I couldn't find you earlier. I wanted to say bye, " said Lina, noticing a huge smile on Eves's face.

"Is everything ok? Your smile is cheek to cheek."

"My parents told me we are moving home." Said Eve.

"That's great, I'm so happy for you. Where are you moving to?" Asks Lina.

"Ananke!" Eve replies.

END

About the Author

Sara Noor is a devoted mother and storyteller with a passion for bringing joy and inspiration to readers of all ages. Through her imaginative tales, Sara aims to show that creativity knows no bounds and that, with a little imagination, anything is possible. Her stories are crafted to entertain and uplift, reminding readers that they have the power to bring their own ideas to life.

Acknowledgments

A heartfelt thank you to my dear friend Maryum, whose friendship has meant the world to me. This novella would not have come to life without the inspiration I found in her wonderful children, Saffiyah, Aisha and Khalid. Their bright smiles, endless curiosity, and boundless imaginations sparked the ideas that shaped this story.

I hope this book has brought as much laughter and adventure to your family as it has to mine.